LULU

THE

BROADWAY
MOUSE

THE SHOW
MUST GO ON

LULU

THE
BROADWAY
MOUSE

THE SHOW
MUST GO ON

JENNA GAVIGAN

RP|KIDS
PHILADELPHIA

• •

Copyright © 2020 by Jenna Gavigan
Cover and interior illustrations copyright © 2020 by Erwin Madrid
Cover copyright © 2020 by Hachette Book Group, Inc.

Running Press Kids
Hachette Book Group
1290 Avenue of the Americas, New York, NY 10104
www.runningpress.com/rpkids
@RP_Kids

Printed in the United States of America

First Edition: March 2020

Published by Running Press Kids, an imprint of Perseus Books, LLC, a subsidiary of Hachette Book Group, Inc. The Running Press Kids name and logo is a trademark of the Hachette Book Group.

The Hachette Speakers Bureau provides a wide range of authors for speaking events. To find out more, go to www.hachettespeakersbureau.com or call (866) 376-6591.

The publisher is not responsible for websites (or their content) that are not owned by the publisher.

Print book cover and interior design by Frances J. Soo Ping Chow.

Library of Congress Control Number: 2019934246

ISBNs: 978-0-7624-9648-8 (hardcover), 978-0-7624-9651-8 (ebook)

LSC-C

10 9 8 7 6 5 4 3 2 1

**FOR MEREDITH,
MY BRAVE (AND FUNNY) FRIEND**

HERE'S THE NEWS

I HAVE SOMETHING TO TELL YOU, DEAR READER. FAIR warning: I might (definitely) cry.

Our show is closing.

I just . . .

I guess I should do as Fraulein Maria advises and "start at the very beginning" so you can understand how we got here. (Once you understand how we got here, if you wouldn't mind explaining it to me, that'd be fab.)

It makes sense that the beginning of this story would pick up where the last one left off, right? (If you just answered, "Of course right!" bravo to you, tiny Yente.) So, although it is currently spring and my fellow cast members have been donning sockless shoes and jean jackets to match the warm breeze blowing through Shubert Alley, let's rewind to the depths of winter, puffy coats, snow boots, and blustery winds, aka a few days after my Broadway debut. Back to when my heart was bursting with joy, pride, exaltation . . . I could continue to list other applicable emotions, but we'd be here all day.

Okay. Here goes everything.

CHAPTER
ONE

"EXTRA! EXTRA! READ ALL ABOUT IT!" TIMMY HOL-lers. At least I think that's what he's hollering. His speech is mumbled because he and my other three hooligan brothers each have their mouths wrapped around a corner of this weekend's massive Arts section of the *Times,* and they're slowly maneuvering it into our house, like they're crew guys moving a cumbersome set piece. Speaking of crew guys, it was Dan and Artie who arrived at work this morning with easily fifty copies of the paper—enough for everyone in the building. They tried to get a copy downstairs to me, but the Hooligans intercepted it. Apparently, Benji said, "We'll take it from here, you clever gentlemen." (In other news, Benji has stopped talking like a cowboy and started talking like a fictional English butler.) Sure, it would have been easier to have a human carry the hefty newspaper downstairs, but my brothers wouldn't hear of it. If I could make it to Broadway, they could certainly handle weekend *Times* transportation.

"Put it down over here, boys, where we can all see it," my mother instructs.

The Hooligans plop the paper down, and my mom smooths it out with her tail. (Five bucks says later she'll ask Bet to iron it before asking one of the carpenters to frame it.)

"May I do the honors?" Timmy asks.

"You are our resident newspaper aficionado," I say.

Timmy clears his throat, then reads, "Shubert Theatre Makes History with Lulu the Broadway Mouse." Right below the headline is a huge photograph of me in Jayne's palm during Act Two, both of us with our left legs in a high kick. After the show, we found out that our sound guy,

Randall, who dabbles in photography, went to the back of the house during Act Two to make sure our debuts were documented. The *Times* bought a bunch of photos from him and now Randall can take that trip to Hawaii he's been dreaming about.

"Wow," Walt says. "That's some headline, Lu."

"The front page of the Arts section," my dad says. "My little girl."

"Everyone told you it wasn't possible," my mother says. "Even me. I'm so glad you didn't listen, Lucy Louise."

"Me too, Mom," I say.

Cut to Benji the Brit "not crying!" beside me.

"Keep reading, bro," Matty says.

The seven of us curl up around the newspaper, and each other, as Timmy continues to read.

On Tuesday evening, toward the end of the first act, a tiny mouse named Lulu made a surprise appearance onstage at the Shubert. By the curtain call, that tiny mouse had become a big star . . .

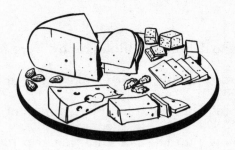

CHAPTER
TWO

Y OU COULDN'T BUY A BETTER HEADLINE!" JODIE
Howard proclaims. "And believe me, I've tried."
She pulls her sand-colored wig cap over her
pin-curled noggin, then turns to me and H.H., suddenly
serious as all get-out. "I'm kidding, of course. I would
never buy a headline."

"Of course you wouldn't," I say.

"This is the kind of article an actor dreams of, Tiny,"
Heather Huffman says. "Are you happy with it?"

"Of course," I say. "I mean, it's great for me, but it's
great for everyone else, too, right?"

"ABSOLUTELY!" Jodie shouts. "Free publicity is

the best publicity!" She dots concealer under her eyes and begins blending with her purple makeup sponge. "We're sold out for both shows today! You've made us a hit again, darling."

"If you had any use for money, I'd say it were time for a raise," H.H. says in that matter-of-fact way she does. "Perhaps there's something else we can negotiate for you? A weekly cheese platter delivery? A cushy new bed? A larger assortment of ribbon scarves?"

"Is it ridiculous to say being allowed to perform is payment enough?" I ask.

The looks on H.H.'s and Jodie's faces confirm that, yes, it is ridiculous, and I realize that me declaring out loud that I don't feel the need to be compensated for my hard work is basically pooh-poohing the strides made by generations of human women. If I'm going to blaze a trail for future generations of thespian mice, I'd better make it clear I know my worth.

"I'll ask for the cheese platter," I say.

"Good," H.H. says, retrieving a brand-new eyeliner—Cup O' Cappuccino—from a reusable Duane Reade tote. "Whatever the ask, if I know one thing for sure, it's that producers never get rid of their cash cow. Or their cash mouse, in this case." She lets out a fluttery laugh. "I think it's safe to say your job is secure, Tiny. Now. Are you sure you're still up for our preshow routine? I'd understand if you need to get up to the third floor and prepare for your own show."

"I will never give up our preshow routine," I say. "You're stuck with me."

"All right then," H.H. says. "My eyelash, please."

I scoot across their dressing room counter; my speed is slowed a bit by H.H.'s scratchy new bamboo place mat—aka her "much-needed touch of Zen." I knock the cover off the lash container, pick up her left lash, and stride it over to her. Just like I've done for three hundred fifty-two performances, just like I'll do for many, many more.

"Not to gossip," Jodie Howard whispers loudly, "but . . .

I am surprised that with Amanda back from her sickbed she hasn't made a fuss about you being her new costar."

"I wasn't going to say anything, but now that you've said something, yes. It is incredibly surprising," H.H. replies.

"Life's surprising," I say.

"Indeed, it is," H.H. says, eyeing me suspiciously before closing her left lid to apply its lash.

Just between us, dear reader, my third-floor dressing room mates and I decided it was best not to broadcast our unanimous decision to turn over a new leaf and get along. We didn't want anyone else's opinions to influence things, you know? Believe me, it's tough for me not to divulge every detail to H.H. But Amanda's confession about why she acted the way she did, and my realization about how we all could have treated her better? We think it's best we keep those experiences between the four of us: me, Milly, Amanda, and Jayne. The hope is the rest of the company will sense our fresh start, without us having to explicitly state "We're going to get along now!" and that jolt of positivity will brighten up our backstage like a fresh coat of paint.

"In other news, I will be missing two performances next week to shoot a television pilot. Guest star. Possible *recurring*. I'm thrilled."

Bless Jodie Howard for her ability to steer the conversation back to her and away from topics that make me feel like I'm lying to my best H.H.

"Which one?" H.H. asks. "The one about the family who owns the bookstore?"

"No," Jodie says. "No, I was deemed 'too wise' for that one." She rolls her eyes and snorts some saline nasal spray. "That's show biz speak for 'too old,' Lulu."

"Got it," I say. I got it before she told me but would never have said it out loud. I mean, how could someone be "too wise" to own a bookstore? Honestly.

"The one about the Nantucket cop who solves crimes with the chef of his local seafood restaurant?" H.H. asks.

How she made it through that description without laughing, I'll never know.

"They said I 'wasn't believable' as someone who 'shucks oysters,'" Jodie says, decorating the statement with her signature air quotes. "No, I booked *Apartment*. Half-hour comedy. Single camera. Very *Downton Abbey* but set on the Upper West Side in a prewar co-op." (FYI, "booked" is show biz speak for getting the part.)

"Sounds fun," H.H. says. And, yes, I do sense a hint of envy that she's doing her best to repress. The gal's only human, ya know?

"Fifteen Minutes, this is your Fifteen-Minute call. Fifteen Minutes, please," Pete's voice pipes through the monitor.

"Congrats on your guest star, possible recurring, Jodie!" I say. "H.H. and I will miss you next week."

"Yes, Lisa is lovely in your role—" H.H. starts.

"I hope not *too* lovely," Jodie panics.

"—but she's not you, my friend. *You* are one of a

kind. And speaking of one of a kind, Tiny, you'd better head upstairs and get ready. We'll see you at the overture dance."

"See you in fifteen!" I say. But before I go, I whisper into her ear, "You'll book a television role soon, H.H. I just know it."

She pats me on the head and says, "From your lips to Casting's ears, Tiny."

And then, faster than you can say "There's no business like show business," I'm off. Down the leg of their dressing room table, out the door to the second-floor hallway, and up the stairs to the third floor and *my* dressing room. *Our* dressing room. Amanda's, Jayne's, Milly's, and mine.

What's that you say? *Do you have your own name plaque on the door yet, Lulu?* Well, right now all I have is a piece of printer paper Milly fashioned into a name plaque. Pete did put a place for me to sign in on the call board, though! Rosa rubs a marker on my foot and then holds me up so I can use my foot as a stamp.

Once it's decided that this part is mine for good, I'm sure Pete will turn the printer paper hanging on our dressing room door into an official name plaque faster than you can say "Please come back to Broadway, Tony winner Kristin Chenoweth."

Oh yes, I forgot to mention. *Technically,* I'm still an understudy. Despite what H.H. said about the producers never getting rid of their cash cow-mouse, despite making the cover of the Arts section of the *Times,* despite five stellar performances, this role isn't technically mine until the producers say it is.

This might be a show, but it's also a business.

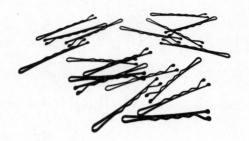

CHAPTER
THREE

L ULU, DO YOU NEED ME TO MAKE ROOM FOR YOU?"
Amanda asks. Nicely.

I'll hold so you can pick your jaw up off the floor.

"No, I'm good," I say. "But thanks for asking."

"Of course," Amanda says. "I want you to feel included."

I look at Jayne and Jayne looks at Milly and Milly just smiles with contented relief. Amanda's trying a bit too hard to be nice, but over-the-top effort is definitely better than zero effort. It's as if someone dialed her nice meter from one to one hundred and now the water's boiling over in her pot and she needs to turn the heat down just a tiny bit so we can land on a rolling bubble and sorry for the mixed metaphor.

"Thanks," I say. "Don't worry. I do."

"I was thinking with the weather as bad as it is, it might be fun to order in Chinese for in between shows," Milly says. "Thoughts?"

"Yes, please!" Jayne says.

"I'm always in the mood for those crunchy noodles that come in the little bag," I say. We mice love a crunchy food. Helps keep our teeth in good shape. The crunchier the better.

"Sure," Amanda says. "I finally have my appetite back."

"We'll look at the menu during intermission," Milly says, practically beaming from how easy that just was.

"Five Minutes, this is your Five-Minute call," Pete's voice commands. "Five Minutes, please."

"Knock, knock," Jeremiah says. "Ready for your wig, Amanda?"

"Of course," she says with a smile. "Come on in."

Jeremiah stands behind Amanda, positioning the wig directly over her head. She reaches up in front of her face, hooks her thumbs under the wig's lace—REAL HUMAN HAIR is hand tied into a lace cap of sorts to form the wig— and Jeremiah glides the wig onto her head. He puts one pin in. A second. A third. Not a peep from Amanda. Until . . .

"Thanks so much, Jeremiah," Amanda says. "I really appreciate it."

"Sure thing," Jeremiah says.

For the record, Amanda's been this nice ever since she returned to the show on Wednesday evening, but I think everyone just assumed the good vibes would wear off faster than the food poisoning did. But so far, so good.

I was, of course, a bit worried about my first performance with Amanda. My first two shows were also Jayne's first two shows, so our only experience performing our roles was with each other. But sharing the stage with Amanda is truly a delight. I doubt I would have felt the same a week ago; a week ago she probably would have twirled me into the orchestra pit. But now that we're friends, things are just fabulous.

"I'll see you after your first exit," Jeremiah says. "Have a good show, ladies."

"You too!" I say. I can't tell you how incredible it feels to know that "Have a good show" truly applies to me, too.

"By the way, Lulu," Jeremiah says, crouching down from his towering height so we're closer to eye level, "that *Times* write-up was really something. So proud of you. You too, Jayne."

"Thanks," Jayne says quickly.

"What *Times* write-up?" Amanda asks.

Jeremiah's eyes go wide and then shut as he emits a soft *guhhhhh,* like he just dropped his cell phone into a sewer grate.

"What *Times* write-up?" Amanda asks again.

"There's a little article in the paper today about Lulu's debut," Milly says. "I just assumed you saw." In truth, we weren't sure whether Amanda had seen it or not, but Milly, Jayne, and I agreed that it was probably best not to bring it up. If Amanda brought it up, fine. But if she didn't, we should forget to mention it. That isn't lying, that's just *omitting*. This doesn't count as us ganging up on her, but I see how you might interpret it that way.

"No, I haven't seen it," Amanda says. "Do you have a copy?"

Had this scene played out a week ago, before we all turned over our new leaves, I'm sure Milly would have come up with some sort of excuse to not show the paper to Amanda. She'd have said, "You know you're not allowed to touch newspapers when you're in your vanilla velvet dress!" or something like that. But today's a new day. So Milly says, "Sure. Here you go," and hands a copy to Amanda.

Jeremiah lingers in the doorway, his head hung in terrified shame like a puppy who gnawed on a brand-new stiletto. Milly, Jayne, and I smile kindly at Amanda as she reads, though I'm certain we're all mentally preparing for the temper tantrum of the century.

"Wow," Amanda says.

Wow can mean anything, Team. *Wow* can mean anything.

"This . . ." she starts.

If need be, I can be out the door and to the safety of H.H.'s "much-needed moment of Zen" mat in under sixty seconds.

"Is . . ." she continues.

Maybe I should preemptively hit the road. Just in case.

"Really wonderful," she says. "How great for you guys."

We all breathe a sigh of relief so grand we practically blow the costumes off their hangers.

"Thanks, Amanda," I say. "That means a lot."

"Yeah," Jayne says. "It really does."

"I'll read the rest later when we're eating our Chinese food," Amanda says.

Here's the thing: I'm sure she's upset. I'm certain. I've known this gal for almost a year. But feeling something is one thing. It's how you respond to that feeling that makes the difference. And Amanda's response is pure class. I'm proud of her. So proud I could whistle. (But I won't. Because just in case you forgot: we never whistle in the theatre.)

"Places for the top of Act One," Pete's voice commands. "This is your Places call. Places, please."

"Let's get this show on the road," Milly says.

And we're off. Down the stairs to the stage for our overture dance. For my first Saturday matinee performance on Broadway. If this is a dream, please don't wake me.

CHAPTER
FOUR

MIND PASSING THE SOUP DUMPLINGS, MILLY?"
Jayne asks.

"With pleasure," Milly says, handing Jayne the piping-hot container of deliciousness.

This is the between-shows feast to end all between-shows feasts. Soup dumplings, veggie chow mein, chicken with broccoli, crunchy noodles, scallion pancakes . . . yummy heaven. I'm actually super surprised the Hooligans haven't—

"Good evening, one and all," Benji the Brit declares.

I spoke too soon. Order food and my brothers *shan't* be far behind.

"What's in those dumplings?" Walt asks, scurrying over to Jayne.

"Soup," she says, her mouth half full. "And pork."

"Sign me up," Walt says, cozying up to Jayne. Benji's eyes go wide. Not because of how delicious the dumplings look (and smell), but because Walt had better back away from Benji's crush faster than Michael Banks got sucked up his 17 Cherry Tree Lane chimney, or some mouse fur is going to fly.

"That's a lot of crunchy noodles, Lu," Matty says. "I can help you finish them if—"

"No help is needed, thank you very much," I say. "Step away from the Chinese food and return from whence you came."

"That's just plain mean," Walt says.

"You weren't invited," I say. "That's just plain *rude*."

"They're welcome to join," Amanda says. This, from the gal who threated to "call the exterminator!" when the show first moved into the building.

"No," I say. "I mean, that's really nice of you, Amanda, but they have plenty of food downstairs."

"Speaking of downstairs," Timmy says, momentarily refocusing his attention away from the crunchy broccoli stems. "Did you see what Pete posted on the call board?"

"No," Jayne says. (P.S. Benji is next to her smiling politely like he's one of Queen Elizabeth's obedient corgis.) "Did someone call out for tonight's show?"

"Call out" is Broadway slang for saying you're not doing the show. So when someone has laryngitis or a pulled muscle or secretly booked a job on a commercial but Pete wouldn't grant them a personal day, they "call out." Calling out for a secret job is against union rules, by the way, and therefore highly unrecommended.

"Nope," Timmy says. "The producers will be in the audience tomorrow."

These words make my stomach hop up into my throat. Because, as you know from a few pages ago, it's the producers who will decide whether or not I permanently take over this track from Teddy the Bear.

Let me get my mind off our producers for a moment; I'll explain to you what a "track" means, in case you don't know. The main difference between a track and a "role" is that some actors play multiple roles. So . . . okay, let's use Harper, who's in our ensemble, as an example. Harper plays a maid, a dinner guest, and a passerby, so saying, "Brittany is going on for Harper's track" means Brittany will play all those roles, just like Harper does. One human is basically taking the place of another human—does that make sense? It's one of those things that seems complicated until you see it in action all the time, then it seems normal and logical and—

Okay. Enough stalling. Back to the producers—aka the people who raise money to put on a show and therefore make a lot of major decisions.

There's only one reason the producers can be seeing

the show tomorrow and that reason is tiny and gray, and has a tail that looks like a witch's finger and a heart full of love for all things musical.

(That reason is me.)

Milly can read me like a best-selling book, so she's fully aware that my mood just went from jovial to jittery. "They're going to love you, Lulu. Just like the audiences do. Just like we do."

"I'm sure it's nothing to worry about," Jayne says. "Not that I'm really an expert on the subject of our producers. I've never even met them."

Amanda's face twitches. It's a slight, subtle movement. But I notice it, and it sets off alarm bells.

"You've never met the producers?" Amanda asks.

"Nope," Jayne says. "Anyone mind if I have the last soup dumpling?"

"Go for it," Milly says.

"How have you never met them?" Amanda asks. "Weren't they at your audition?"

"Pete and a casting associate put me on tape," Jayne mumbles, mouth full of broth.

"It was all a bit quick," Milly says. "Maya giving her notice and all. They couldn't find a date where all the producers and Samantha could be in New York so they watched a tape of Jayne's audition instead."

I can't take my eyes off of Amanda. She's working so hard to seem nonchalant, easy breezy, okay with it all. I can tell this news of the producers never having seen Jayne perform in person is worrying her, but I don't understand why.

"I need to go wash my hands," Amanda says. "They're covered in chicken and broccoli. Be right back." She heads out the door and down the hallway to our tiny bathroom, even though there's a perfectly good sink right here in the dressing room, plus jumbo-sized bottles of hand sanitizer.

"I'm going to go make sure she's okay," I say.

"Good idea," Milly says. "Thanks."

Before I go, I look at my brothers; I make eye contact with each of them. Serious, focused eye contact so they know I'm not playing around. "There are currently seven crunchy noodles left in this bag. You may each eat one. That leaves three. Three crunchy noodles for me. If fewer than three crunchy noodles remain upon my return, I will tell Mom and Dad precisely how that king-sized Snickers ended up in our nest. Understand?"

My brothers nod. And I head out to see what's up with Amanda.

(P.S. I have no idea how that king-sized Snickers ended up in our nest; that's called improv, baby.)

———————◇———————

"AMANDA?" I SCRATCH AT THE DOOR BECAUSE THOUGH I defied all odds to become the first mouse to perform on Broadway, there's really no hope of me and my meager limbs ever producing a substantial knock.

"I'll be right out," she calls. I hear her turn on the

sink to keep up with her *I left the room because my hands are covered in Chinese food, not because I didn't want anyone to see me cry* story.

"Okay . . . ," I say. "I'm here if you want to talk." I scale up the painted concrete wall to the windowsill directly across from the bathroom. As I wait for Amanda to emerge, I watch the snow fall down onto Shubert Alley. This really is a dreamy place to call home.

When the door opens, Amanda's smiling brightly.

"Why would I need to talk?" she asks. "I'm fine."

"It's okay if you aren't," I say.

Amanda walks over to me and the windowsill. Funny, when this show first moved into the theatre, I remember Amanda having to stand on her tippy-toes to look out this window. Now, if someone down in the alley looked up, they'd see not only her head but her shoulders, too. Over this last almost year, she's sprouted up faster than you can say "Billy Porter upcycled the *Kinky Boots* curtain into an outfit for the 2019 Tony

Awards and if that isn't resourceful and chic I don't know what is."

"It's stupid," she says.

"Just because you wish you weren't feeling a certain way doesn't mean you shouldn't be feeling that way," I say. "You can tell me anything."

"The producers haven't seen Jayne in person," Amanda says.

"Keep going . . . ," I say.

"Maybe that's why they're coming tomorrow," Amanda says.

"But she's not performing tomorrow," I say. "You are." *I am*, I think. If they're here to see anyone, they're here to see me, and though I'm able to dish out advice to Amanda faster than my brothers just ("Accidentally!") finished that entire bag of crunchy noodles, I'm having trouble dishing it out to myself.

"You don't have anything to worry about, Lulu," Amanda says.

"How did you know I was worried?" I ask.

"You get a little crinkle between your eyes. Makes your fur scrunch up," Amanda says.

"Oh," I say. Amanda knows me. I had no idea.

"You don't have anything to worry about because the audiences love you. We're sold out tonight. You're our new star."

"I hate to quibble, but Stella's name is the one sparkling up on our marquee and it always will be. Hence, she's the star," I say. (Though it *is* nice to hear someone call me a star.)

"You know what I mean," Amanda says. "You're a draw. You're why the audiences are showing up. I'm old news."

"You're twelve," I say. "Far from old."

"Well, I may not be old, but I'm definitely tall," she says, looking down at her yoga pants, which were once full length and are now closer to capris.

"Everyone's tall compared to me," I say.

"I'm serious, Lulu," Amanda says. "There's a very good

chance they'll take one look at Jayne and one look at me and realize she's more right for the role now."

Instead of throwing out another cheery distraction of a sentence, I decide to face facts. "I guess it's possible," I say. "Yes, you have gotten taller. Yes, Jayne is much smaller. But all of that is out of your control. All you can do is give a great show tomorrow, like you always do."

Amanda smiles at me. It's genuine this time. It's not forced, it's not for show. "I really like performing with you," Amanda says.

"I really like performing with you, too," I say.

"I was a little worried you'd rather be with Jayne," Amanda says. "Since you made your debuts together."

"We made our debuts together thanks to you," I say. Suddenly, tears sprout in my eyes. "I never thanked you, you know."

"I wasn't exactly supportive of you," Amanda says. "You shouldn't be thanking me."

"But I am," I say.

"Well, then, you're welcome," Amanda says. "And thank you for the pep talk."

"You're welcome, my friend," I say.

Amanda. My friend. First, I make my Broadway debut, then Amanda and I become friends? Neither of these happenings was likely to occur. If I were superstitious (and, duh, I am), I would say things come in threes, and I'd warn you, dear reader: be prepared for number three to be a doozy.

CHAPTER
FIVE

I T WAS A GOOD SHOW, WASN'T IT?" AMANDA WHIS-
pers to me.

She and I are offstage right, waiting to bow, and
I'm looking at her like she's nuts. Because my first Sunday
show and the last performance of my first week on Broadway was . . . exhilarating. Sublime. Off-the-charts nailing
it. A full house, a split track in the ensemble (which
means one of our swings, Brittany—who I mentioned
earlier—performed the tracks of two members of our
ensemble, all on her own), and an especially energized
performance from the entire company (thanks to our producers sitting fifth row center on the aisle) made for a

dream of a show. (A "swing," by the way, is a performer who understudies a bunch of other performers and their respective tracks. Brittany, for example, understudies all eight female ensemble members. Hmmm . . . all of these definitions are making me think a glossary of terms might be useful. Stay tuned.)

"It was a *spectacular* show," I say. "You were fabulous. That high note at the end of your final number was incredible."

"Was it?" Amanda asks. She's not fishing for compliments, Team. She's genuinely worried the show didn't go well. Wasn't she there?!

"Weren't you there?" I ask.

"I've done this show so many times I feel like I can't really tell anymore," she says.

"Well, I've only done it a few times, so I was very much there, and I can say with certainty that today was one of your best shows ever, Amanda."

"Thanks," she says. The trombone slides in the way

it does to cue our entrance for bows and Amanda says, "Let's go."

Amanda runs out—I'm in her palms—and when she lands center stage she opens her palms and presents me to the audience. Instant standing ovation. Instant. Even the—for the love of Kander and Ebb—THE PRODUCERS ARE STANDING.

H.H. and Jodie Howard were right. Milly and Jayne were right. I had nothing to worry about.

Stella strides out after us and bows like the legend she is. If the producers were cartoon characters, they'd have gold stars darting out of and around their eyes. I'm surprised they aren't hurling roses at her like they did on opening night. They're thrilled. I can tell. Believe me, I know when humans *aren't* thrilled. When humans aren't thrilled, it's my cue to run.

Amanda plops me in H.H.'s pocket—this has been our bow choreography since my opening night—and I feel the company bend to take a group bow. I feel the lights, I hear the applause, and a sense of contentment and peace washes over me. I'm where I'm supposed to be. I just know it. In the words of Dolly Levi (protagonist of *Hello, Dolly!*), "I'm stayin' where I'm at, fellas!"

———————◇———————

THE PRODUCERS DIDN'T COME UP TO MEET ME, SO I'M pretty certain I'm doomed.

"It doesn't mean anything," Pete says. Milly summoned Pete because I "wasn't listening to reason." Neither was Amanda. She's been anxiously brushing out her pin curls for the last five minutes and she's starting to look like she stuck her finger in an electrical socket. "It's Sunday evening. They have auditions for another show bright and early tomorrow morning. I'm sure they were just eager to get home."

"But what did they *say*?" Amanda asks. She's toeing the line between the whiny Amanda of yesteryear and the *everything's fine!* Amanda of yesterday, and frankly this combo seems like the most honest version of herself. A nice, sensible 50/50.

"They said the show is in great shape and they're thrilled," Pete says.

"That's all?" I ask. Humbly, I was hoping for a "That mouse is a wonder!" or a "We're commissioning the *Dear Evan Hansen* team to write Lulu her very own musical, which we're certain will win the Tony and will subsequently be turned into an Academy Award–winning movie!" but frankly I would have settled for a "What's-her-name the mouse did a decent job and I guess we'll keep her."

"They didn't say anything specific about anyone," Pete says.

"Not even me?" Jayne asks.

"What's that supposed to mean?" Amanda asks. Okay, now she's 65 percent old Amanda, 35 percent new, and I'm a teensy bit nervous.

"It was a joke," Jayne says, zipping up her massive backpack. "Because I was up here the whole show doing a book report on *Number the Stars* and they probably don't even know I exist."

"They know you exist," Pete says. And as quickly as he says it, I can tell he regrets it.

"What's *that* supposed to mean?" Amanda demands. We are now at 80 percent old Amanda and 20 percent new Amanda, and I'm not going to lie to you, Team, I'm scared.

"They know everyone exists," Pete says. "Jayne in here, Artie and Dan up in the flies, Bet down in wardrobe. They know about everyone."

"We're all in this together!" Milly says like the cheerleader atop the pyramid. (Or like the kids in *High School Musical*. Good catch, dear reader. Good catch.) "Let's get you girls down to the stage door. Your parents are probably frozen solid out in the alley."

As the girls throw on their winter coats and wrap thick scarves around their necks—it's very important we singers protect our instruments—I hear Amanda whisper to Jayne, "I'm sorry. I didn't mean to overreact."

"Apology accepted," Jayne says. "I'm sorry I made an insensitive joke."

Milly hears this scene, too, and I see her body relax back to how it was yesterday between shows. Back to when we were eating Chinese food and things were peaceful and all we had to worry about was who would get the last soup dumpling. Back to before the producers confused us with their mixed messages: a standing ovation followed by no visit up to our dressing room.

"Have a nice day off, ladies," Pete says.

"Pete, am I . . . ?" I start.

"Are you what?" Pete asks.

I'm almost too scared to ask. But tomorrow will be a torturous day of worry and wonder if I don't know it's mine. For real. My role. For keeps. Holy cannoli, no wonder Jodie and H.H. swore never to be understudies ever again. The weight of this uncertainty is far too heavy to carry.

"Am I on? On Tuesday, I mean."

"Is it permanently your role, you mean?" Pete asks.

"No offense to Teddy the Bear," Jayne says, "but Lulu's better in the part."

"I agree," Amanda says, topping off her outfit with fluffy earmuffs. "I far prefer performing with Lulu." I never thought I'd say this, but: BLESS YOU, AMANDA.

"I wish I could tell you you're in the track forever," Pete says. "But the producers and I have a meeting on Tuesday and I'm guessing that's one of the things we'll discuss."

And with just a handful of words, Pete pops my balloon. He popped it and sad confetti flew out and now it's all over the floor like a sad, sad mess.

"I will say this, though"—Pete turns to face me square on, like he always does when he has something serious to tell me—"the rise in ticket sales directly correlates with your debut, Lulu. This I know. Of this, I will remind them. I promise you."

"Thanks, Pete," I say. "I'm sure it will . . ." No. I refuse to say I'm sure it will work out. Because it's very possible it won't. It's very possible that despite this weekend's sold-out houses, despite the glowing article in the *Times*, despite the sage certainty of H.H. and Jodie Howard, our producers might decide that a mouse on Broadway is not for them. *I'm* not for them. That it's all too much, too different, too far from the norm. That this was a fun experiment, but the results show that watching a mouse sing and dance on Broadway is just too much for most theatregoers to handle. And I might be headed back to my old roles: backstage cheerleader, coach, friend. Wannabe.

I honestly can't say which is worse: dreaming of Broadway forever, or having to say goodbye to it after only a week. But I can say which is best: doing this show over and over and over again. That's the best.

CHAPTER
SIX

I COULD USE SOME HELP REPAIRING THIS DRESS, if you're looking for a distraction," Bet says, holding up a costume with a tear in its underarm.

"Stella did that during the finale," I say. "I heard the rip." Because I was there. Right there next to Stella, singing my heart out and smiling like I had finally gotten the thing I'd wished for my entire life.

But that was Sunday. Today is Tuesday. The day of reckoning. The day of the big reveal. The day of Pete's meeting with our producers. I'm so nervous I could puke all over, but because Amanda did that only a mere week ago, I will spare the wardrobe room another mess and let this anxiety fester in my body like—

Yes, I know I'm being dramatic. I do.

I will try to be sensible.

I will try to calm down. If *you'll* try to think of the one thing you've wanted your whole life. Got that thing? Okay. Good. Now, think of what would happen if you achieved that thing—that dream, if you will—and then think of how you'd feel if in mere hours, maybe even minutes or seconds, you were finding out the fate of that dream. Finding out if it was just beginning, or if it was already over.

You feel like you want to vomit dramatics, right? Thought so.

"I'm worried about you, Lucy Louise," my mom says. She's using the wax from a birthday candle to unstick a zipper. My mother is a crafty wizard. "You look gray."

"I always look gray," I say with a wink. (Cuz I'm a mouse. And we're gray.)

"You know what I mean," she says, looking at me with her signature *I know what you look like because I made you* look. "Whatever happens today, you know it has nothing to do with you or your talent."

"What does it have to do with then?" I ask.

"Politics," Bet says. "Also, rules, worry, fear. . . . This business is far too complicated, Lulu. You know that. It's a ridiculous, horrible—"

"Wonderful!" I interject.

"—wonderful business, yes that, too," Bet says. "I've seen all sides of it over these last seventy years. There's no point in trying to apply reason to madness."

"I guess," I say.

I hear a *knock, knock,* and . . . it's Pete! IT'S PETE. I have never in my life felt this combination of thrill and terror upon seeing a human. Not even when Stella had cream puffs delivered to celebrate our hundredth show and my brothers got wayyyy too close to the delivery guy.

"What's the scoop?" I ask. P.S. I'm shocked at my

ability to produce a simple yet sassy sentence, despite the fact that I'm more nervous than I was that time Susie's sister showed up with a cat in a stroller. Adrenaline is a wonder.

"I'm only telling you this because I know how worried you've been," Pete says.

P.P.S. My mother has found her way over to me and has me enveloped in an *it's going to be okay* hug.

"The meeting wasn't about you," Pete says.

"What?" I ask. For the love of Rodgers & Hammerstein, what does that even mean?!

"I asked about you, of course," Pete says. "And they said . . ."

I'm floating over my body looking down at this scene, looking down at my tiny body—my tiny body that's both tense and limp at the same time—and I'm meditating on what I hope Pete will say. I won't dare reveal my meditative wish, for fear it won't come true. But you know what it is, dear reader. Or you don't know me at all.

"The role is yours," Pete says.

I'm back in my body and my body is sobbing.

"Oh, sweetheart," my mom says. "Oh, honey, I'm so happy for you."

"Sorry," I say to Pete. "Sorry I'm crying."

"Don't be sorry," Pete says. "Witnessing moments like this is the best part of my job."

"Mine too," Bet says. She's dabbing at her eyes with a handkerchief that's so old, I almost wonder if she's had it since she started work here in 1944. That handkerchief has seen a lot of moments like this. What a lucky handkerchief.

"Wait," I say. "If the meeting wasn't about me, then what was it about?"

"I really shouldn't say," Pete says.

"It's Amanda, isn't it?" I ask.

Though I'm ashamed to admit it, I'd venture to guess that a week ago most people in this building would have been happy to see Amanda go. This *mouse* certainly would have been happy to see her go. But now? Now things are different. Now we're part of the same team. What a difference a week can make. Combine food poisoning, a heart-to-heart, and a few performances side by side and you've got yourself a whole different ballgame. (This sports reference is brought to you commercial-free by my love for my dad.)

"Her contract is up and she's just too tall," Pete says. "We called her agents an hour ago, so I'm guessing that by now, she knows."

"When's her last show?" I ask.

"Four weeks from last Sunday," Pete says. "It'll give us time to find a replacement for Jayne."

"Does that mean . . . ?"

"Jayne's taking over," Pete says. "That was always the plan."

"Well," my mother says, "there's the rainbow after the rain."

"Today is going to be tricky," Pete says. "And I really shouldn't have told you anything other than that your role is safe, so please do your best to act surprised when the girls arrive in a few hours."

"I will," I say.

Pete turns to head out, then stops in the doorway of the wardrobe room and says, "Congratulations, Lulu the Broadway Mouse."

"Thank you, Pete," I say. "I won't let you down."

"Of this, I am certain," he says.

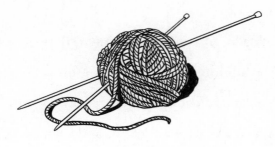

CHAPTER
SEVEN

H I," Jayne says, lingering in the doorway of our dressing room.

"Hi," Amanda replies. She's sitting in her dressing room chair, her hair pin-curled and wig cap on. No makeup yet, though, because this poor girl has been crying since the moment she walked through the stage door, and I can't say I blame her.

Milly's sitting on the floor quietly knitting a sweater for her dog, I'm in her lap holding her lavender yarn, and we're both doing our best not to break out into snotty, heaving sobs.

"I'm so sorry, Amanda," Jayne says.

A week ago, Amanda would have snapped back with a nasty "You should be sorry, you treasonous traitor!" but the evolved Amanda of today doesn't say a word. Instead, she gets up, walks over to Jayne, and collapses into her arms. Like an oak tree falling into a forsythia bush.

Milly and I succumb to snotty, heaving sobs after all, which match Amanda's and Jayne's. Sweet Jayne, who just hours ago was given the best news of her life, is crying so hard I'm worried she might break in two. She's a good soul, our Jayne.

We're all four of us holding each other like Jack and Rose did just as the *Titanic* began to be sucked into the ocean. The theatre does this to you, Team. It holds your heart in its beautifully lit, spectacularly orchestrated hand. You give it your heart gladly, because the love you feel for it is so true and so visceral and so boundless that you're willing to risk sudden death in a cold and icy ocean in exchange for the small chance that you'll be rescued, brought ashore, and live happily ever after.

(Last night I watched *Titanic* up on the fly floor, for comfort. Matty's super skilled when it comes to Dan and Artie's Apple TV.)

"This is ridiculous," Amanda manages. "I'm being ridiculous."

"You are not being ridiculous," Jayne says.

"You're feeling your feelings," I add.

Amanda hiccups out a laugh, mid-sob. "I'm 'feeling my feelings,'" she says. "I like that, Lulu. I might take that with me when I go."

"Take it," I say. "With my love."

"You girls are just so wonderful," Milly says. "I am so, so proud of you, and I love you very, very much."

We take another thirty seconds or so, just holding each other, breathing deeply in unison, and then we pull apart like a sticky bun. We each go our own way, but we'll always, *always* be a part of one another.

Amanda's smartwatch rings "The Lullaby of Broadway" from *42nd Street,* indicating it's fifteen minutes to Half Hour, aka forty-five minutes to Places. "Well, I'd better get going with my makeup," Amanda says. "Can't break my routine with only thirty-two shows left."

Jayne grabs a washcloth; the little white name tag sewn into its seam indicates that it's hers. (This is Bet's and my mom's way of keeping the laundry organized; it's a fairly common practice in the laundry land of Broadway.) Jayne turns on the faucet and runs the washcloth under cold water. Then she squeezes it out and hands it to Amanda. "Put this over your eyes for a few minutes. It'll take the puffiness down. My mom did the same for me when I cried for three hours after not booking the *Sound of Music* tour."

"Which part?" Amanda asks, gratefully accepting the makeshift ice pack. (I'm so glad she asked because *I* was about to ask, because, well . . . you know me and my obsession with *The Sound of Music*, but then I stopped myself because it seemed like terrible timing.)

"Brigitta," Jayne replies with a wistful sigh. (I knew it. She'd be the perfect Brigitta.)

"Well, I'm glad you didn't get it," Amanda says. "If you had, we would never have met."

"I would never have taken your job, you mean," Jayne says.

"We would never have become friends," Amanda says.

(Milly is literally hiccupping proud sobs into her vintage *Full House* thermos, and my goodness, she is going to make a great mom someday.)

"And you didn't take my job," Amanda says. "I just outgrew it." And then, in a very dramatic, old Hollywood kind of way, she drapes the washcloth over her eyes and croons, "And I don't want to hear another word about it."

CHAPTER
EIGHT

T INY, BE A DEAR AND HAND ME A TISSUE," H.H. says.

"Here you go," Lisa says, plucking a tissue from its box before I can even take my first step across the dressing room table. She shoves it at H.H. with a terrifyingly chipper grin. "No need to bother yourself, Lulu."

"How kind," H.H. replies. She delicately captures the tissue, like it's poisoned or something, then juts out her bottom teeth in a move so subtle, only I notice. It's her *I'm not enjoying myself* tell. Lisa (full name Lisa Logan; real name? No idea) is Jodie's understudy, and while Jodie's off doing her "guest spot, possible recurring" on *Apartment,* Lisa's on for both shows today and Thursday evening's.

We're three minutes into Half Hour and Lisa has made this room her own. She's spread out her personal place mat, which sports the surprisingly unpleasant scent of Downy fabric softener and almond coffee creamer. (She spilled her coffee after being startled by the sound of her own cell phone ringing.) While H.H. was in the bathroom, Lisa moved H.H.'s tissues to the other side of the dressing room counter for a reason unbeknownst to us all. And she's . . . peppy. Miss America Pageant peppy. Well-meaning, but still . . . a lot. And before you tell me that Jodie Howard is also a lot, let me clarify. Jodie is a circus and she acknowledges it. Lisa is a circus and she's trying to make it seem like she's a yoga retreat, which only makes her more of a circus.

And H.H.? H.H. isn't having it.

"Oopsie," Lisa says as she accidentally pops the lid

off of a pencil sharpener, spilling curls of eyeliner every-where. "This must be broken."

"It's 'temperamental,'" I say, throwing air quotes around the word like Jodie always does. "That's why Jodie keeps it on the *don't use* area of her dressing room table." (FYI, understudies technically aren't supposed to use the gadgets belonging to the actor they're going on for. Before the show, a dresser from the wardrobe department will move an understudy's personal makeup, brushes, and all that jazz into the dressing room of the role they'll be performing, so they're able to use their own things. Why Lisa felt she could use Jodie's sharp-ener is beyond me. This is her third Broadway show. She really should know better.)

"Well isn't that silly!" Lisa says, with the brightness of a bouquet of corner-deli daisies that have been dyed a color blue that doesn't exist in nature. "Why keep some-thing if it doesn't work?"

Then she tosses the sharpener in the trash.

Oh.

Boy.

Here. We. Go.

"Lisa. Dear," H.H. purrs. "Kindly remove that sharpener from the trash and put it back up on the counter where it belongs."

"But it doesn't work!" Lisa chirps.

"That is entirely beside the point," H.H. says. "It doesn't belong to you, it belongs to Jodie. When she returns on Friday and goes looking for her spare sharpener—"

"Her spare sharpener that doesn't work," Lisa says again, like she's talking to a toddler who needs to hear for a second time that he shouldn't put the remote control in his mouth.

"The sharpener belongs here!" H.H. snaps.

(Oohhh, the sharpener is a metaphor for Jodie Howard. Copy that.)

"There's no need to get testy," Lisa says. "Here. It's back up on the counter. Where it belongs."

"I'll just pull this piece of used mic tape off of it," I say. "There. Good as new." I smile at H.H. in the hope that my sheer presence in the room will prevent her from (perhaps literally) biting Lisa's head off.

"Thank you," H.H. says. She takes a breath, then says, "Tiny. My eyelash, please."

I scurry over to her lashes, and, I swear to you on the heaven that is the original Broadway cast recording of *The Light in the Piazza*, before I can knock the lid off the box of lashes, Lisa picks them up and says, "Here you go."

H.H. flexes her right hand, then quickly retracts it into a fist. Holy *Mean Girls*, she isn't really going to hit Understudy Lisa Logan, is she? A move like that would warrant a write-up in the show report, which would be delivered to Actors' Equity and the producers, and that could mean trouble for my best H.H. I've got to put a stop to this.

"H.H.," I say, "would you mind running down to my

nest for me? I left my chartreuse ribbon scarf and I need it for the show."

She looks at me with eyes so saucy and glistening I can't tell if she's thankful or livid that I stopped her from physically assaulting Understudy Lisa Logan.

"Of course," H.H. says. "Let's you and I go together, just in case I can't find it." She opens her palms and I hop into them.

"I'll be here!" Lisa says. In case we were(n't) wondering.

H.H. opens her mouth to reply, but at this point she's too exasperated to speak, so instead she just gives up and grand exits out of there.

———◇———

"That woman is a menace," H.H. says, plopping me onto what at this point we might as well call *my* windowsill up on the third floor. (Side note: my chartreuse ribbon scarf is safe and sound in my dressing room, and sometimes little white lies are okay.)

"She's just excited to be going on," I say. "She's only been on twice and that was months ago."

"Did she behave this way last time?" H.H. asks. "Did I block it all out?"

"She was more genuinely nervous last time. This time she's overcompensating and trying to pretend she's not nervous," I say, like the amateur psychoanalyst I am. "My guess? She heard Jayne is being moved into Amanda's part and she's hopeful the same will happen to her, if Jodie leaves."

H.H. looks at me and softens a bit. "How did you get so wise, Tiny?"

"Well, my mom and dad, for one thing," I say. "Also, you. My show mom."

"I see," H.H. says, her eyes reddening like the time she accidentally mistook Vicks VapoRub for her Icelandic undereye cream.

"So, if you don't mind, here's a spoonful of wisdom," I say. "I owe you, after all. You've given me a cupful."

"Excellent metaphor," H.H. says. "I'm all ears."

"Jodie's not going anywhere," I say. "Even if this TV pilot becomes a TV series, she'll stick around. You know her; she'll manage to get it all done."

"I suppose," H.H. says.

"Lisa isn't so bad," I say. "She's just eager."

"She could be worse, I suppose," H.H. says. "She could have spilled oil and not coffee."

"And then lit a match," I say.

We giggle together, like the surprisingly perfect pair we are, and H.H. says, "I don't know what I'd do without you, Tiny. I really don't."

"Back at ya, H.H.," I say.

We hear the pitter-patter of slippered feet make their way down the hall, and up walks Jayne, adorable in linen overalls and a turtleneck. "Heather! We never see you up here! Everything okay?"

"I needed a break, and now I'm better," H.H. says. "By the way, Jayne, yesterday I neglected to congratulate you on your upcoming promotion. I'm thrilled for you, absolutely thrilled."

"Thanks," Jayne says. She turns her gaze toward our dressing room door and then back to me and H.H. "I'm just . . . I'm trying not to make too big of a deal about it, you know? For Amanda's sake."

"You young ladies," H.H. says, plucking me off my windowsill and handing me to Jayne, "you give me hope for the future. You're kind, you're thoughtful. You get it."

"Thanks," Jayne says, sitting me on her shoulder.

"Heading back downstairs?" I ask.

"The show must go on," H.H. says. "Thank you for the pep talk, Tiny."

"You're very welcome," I say.

"Fifteen Minutes," Pete's voice croons. "This is your Fifteen-Minute call. Fifteen Minutes, please."

"I'd better hurry," H.H. says, already halfway down the stairs. "Have a good show, ladies."

"Have a good show!" Jayne and I reply in unison.

Then Jayne turns to me and says, "I was coming to find you for a reason. Guess what?"

"What?" I ask.

Jayne scoots us into the bathroom and locks the door. "It's sort of gossip, so I don't want anyone to hear." She plops me onto the sink and takes a seat on the lid of the toilet. We're practically face-to-face, which shows you how small our bathroom is.

"Smart move," I say. "Bad gossip or good gossip?"

"Interesting gossip," Jayne says. "They're holding auditions for my replacement on Tuesday afternoon. In the lower lobby."

"The lower lobby?" I say. "What is this, 1960?" (Back in the day, Broadway auditions used to be held in Broadway theatres. Dreamy, right?)

"I know," Jayne says. "Super old school. I've never actually had an audition in a theatre. They're always in rehearsal studios on Eighth Avenue."

"How'd you find out?" I ask. I'm not going to lie;

if Pete told Jayne before he told me, I am going to be a teensy bit hurt. I'll get over it, but still.

"My agent. Her client has an audition," Jayne says. "Apparently, they're only seeing five girls, which is why they're able to bring them to the theatre. Susie will go through a few dance sequences with them, Michael will have them sing, and Pete will watch them do the scene work."

"What about the producers?" I ask. The producers who I've yet to meet. The producers who, bless them, let me keep my job but have no interest in meeting me, which is . . . *fine*.

"Ricardo's just recording all of the auditions," Jayne says. "Think he and Pete will let us watch?"

"Doubtful," I say.

"Well . . ." Jayne starts. "I doubt I could convince my mom to bring me to the theatre that early anyway, because it would involve me missing school. So you'll have to spy on auditions for the both of us!"

"Done," I say.

Jayne turns on the sink and washes her hands, just to keep up with the charade. Then she pops me in one of the front pockets of her overalls and we head down the hallway so I can get ready for our two-show day.

CHAPTER
NINE

I KNOW YOU'RE GOING TO SPY ON AUDITIONS, SO I might as well preemptively give you permission," Pete says. He pushes his glasses up the bridge of his nose right after he says "permission." This, dear reader, is what we show folk call a "button": a physical cue that a musical number or scene is at its end, like how a button is the final thing you do to your jacket, before you walk out the door. An example of a button you might be familiar with is at the end of *Wicked*'s "One Short Day." The "Boo!" "Ahh!" = a button. There are so, so many examples. Start keeping an eye and ear out for them. Timing really is everything.

"I'm not going to argue with you," I say. A piece of advice? Take wins when they're handed to you.

"While I'm sure the girls auditioning today have heard all about Lulu the Broadway Mouse, I'd rather them not see you. It's not really professional to have cast members watch auditions," Pete says.

"I completely agree," I say. (Side note: can we discuss how casually Pete referred to me as a *cast member*?!) "How about I watch from the corner of the bar? I doubt they'll see me, but I'll be able to see them."

(I may or may not have forced my brothers to pretend to be young actresses auditioning for Jayne's track in order to test sight lines this morning. Okay, back to Pete.)

"That sounds like a good plan, Lulu," Pete says, sipping coffee out of his BEST DAD EVER mug. "I'm excited to hold auditions in the theatre. It'll be like the old days. Things were better back then. Simpler. An actor would just show up, wait in line, and they'd get to audition. Period."

"Unless they were a mouse," I say.

"Unless they were a mouse, yes," Pete says. "You fixed that. Your ancestors are somewhere looking down on you and they're very proud. You paved the way for future generations."

If I allowed myself to succumb to the tears that just formed in my throat, I'd fill a teaspoon in under a minute.

"They'll be arriving any second," Susie says, striding in wearing character shoes, warm-up attire, and a *Christmas Carol* baseball cap. (She was in the Madison Square Garden production for, like, a decade.) "We ready?"

Ricardo walks in behind her, scarfing down an egg and cheese on a roll. Show people are funny. They seem to eat breakfast whenever their day begins, be it eight in the morning or three in the afternoon. I'm half expecting Susie to whip out a cup of oatmeal. (My brothers will take care of all crumbs later, no worries.)

"Think I'll put the camera here," Ricardo says. He screws his iPhone into a tripod and plops it on top of the bar.

"I figure we'll dance them, make cuts if necessary—"

I interrupt Pete. "Wait. What?"

"If it's clear one of them can't handle the dance, there's no need to have them sing and read," Susie says, with the coolness of a cucumber who's performed at Radio City, Madison Square Garden, and five Broadway theatres.

"Oh," I say.

There's no need to have them sing and read? Hearing this gives me pause, so, let's . . . pause, while we discuss this. I have very little experience with auditioning. And by "little," I mean zero. But. I have heard audition story after audition story. Everything from being cut at an open call for not having the right "look," to learning twenty pages of music and only being asked to sing sixteen bars, to going through four rounds of callbacks only to lose the role to a celebrity who's never performed onstage. I've heard it all, and the only way to sum it all up is to say: auditioning can be terrible. To the performer, it seems that their feelings are the last thing the people doing the casting are thinking about, because those people are so focused on getting the casting over and done with and done well. But Susie, Pete, and Ricardo aren't your run-of-the-mill casting people, and this isn't a regular audition. I feel, in this moment, that I must speak up for my fellow performers.

"It's just . . . listen. I know it's not my place to say, and I know I've never actually auditioned before, but . . ."

Pete slides his glasses back down the bridge of his nose. "Go ahead, Lulu."

"It's just . . . I heard through the rumor mill that these girls have known about this audition since last week. That probably means they've been rehearsing nonstop since then; they've been going over and over it, probably even in their sleep. If I had been rehearsing for five days, and then wasn't even asked to perform what I had rehearsed . . ."

"This is kind of how it's done, Lulu," Ricardo says, crumpling up his egg and cheese wrapper and tossing it into the garbage can with an actual *swoosh* sound.

(Which, awesome, fulfills my sports viewing quota for the month.)

"I know that's normally how it's done," I say. "But no one from Casting is here. You guys are running this, so can't you make an exception? Treat these girls the way you'd want to be treated if you were the ones auditioning?"

Hearing this makes the expressions on all three of their faces shift slightly.

"Auditions are what turned me from an actor into a stage manager," Ricardo says.

"You were an actor?" I ask.

"I studied Meisner," Ricardo says. "That's *Mice-ner*, to you." (This joke officially qualifies Ricardo for fatherhood.)

"I don't miss auditioning," Susie says. "Cut after cut after cut, hour after hour in crowded dance studios . . ." She stares off into the distance, like she's envisioning a room full of mirrors and long-legged dancers all desperate for a job. (Please, theatre gods, please let Susie break into "The Music and the Mirror" from *A Chorus Line!*)

"My daughter's about to graduate from Carnegie Mellon," Pete says, sighing exhaustedly at the idea that someday someone might cut his daughter before she's given the chance to sing and read simply because her double pirouette wasn't up to par. He pushes his glasses back up his nose and says, "Let's dance them all together, then we'll bring them upstairs one by one to do the scene work at the back of the house and sing with Michael in the pit. Lulu, you're welcome to join if you can find a place to stay out of sight."

If I can find a place? The Hooligans and I scoped out a dozen no-one-will-see-me areas around the theatre to prepare for this afternoon, but it's adorable that Pete thinks otherwise.

"Pete, you have visitors at the stage door," Rosa's voice chirps through the lower lobby's speakers.

"I'll get them," Susie says. Her legs are so long I swear she gets to the lobby stairs in three turned-out strides.

"Here we go," Pete says. "Places, Lulu."

I tuck in behind the bar, and before you can say "Give Julie Andrews a Tony already!" five girls—all wayyyyy shorter than Amanda—parade into the lower lobby, just one shoe change away from auditioning for a Broadway show.

CHAPTER
TEN

J AYNE WHIRLS INTO OUR DRESSING ROOM AND
flings off her coat. "Tell me everything about the
auditions. Don't leave anything out." Then she
remembers that Amanda exists and she quickly says,
"Sorry. So sorry. Super inconsiderate of me."

"It's fine," Amanda says. "I want to hear, too. Spill,
Lulu."

A heavenly breeze of butter and salt wafts into the
room, and in pops Milly carrying a bowl full of freshly
popped popcorn. "Snacks felt appropriate for the occa-
sion," she says. (Side note: the verb "to pop" also felt
appropriate.) "I can't wait to hear about auditions!"

The gals sit side by side, with Milly in the middle and the popcorn on her lap, and they face me, ready to hear all about the two hours I spent this afternoon watching five girls (all under the age of eleven!) audition their hearts out in the hope of making it to Broadway.

"Okay," I say. "Let me start off with a bit of an anticlimactic spoiler alert: I do not know who they hired."

"Well, of course not," Amanda says, with just a teensy bit of her old know-it-all vibe sneaking out. "The producers and Samantha still have to sign off."

"Exactly," I say, blowing past the know-it-all tone because, let's be honest, girls are far too often accused of being know-it-alls when we're actually just correct. "But . . . I do have a guess as to who they're going to hire."

"Ooohhh," Jayne says. "Okay. Names first, please. Let's see if we know any of them."

"Okay," I say. "Ready?"

My three pals nod and pop popcorn into their mouths. At this very moment, they resemble excited pigeons.

"Okay. Penelope Ford, Emilia Rose Mintzer—"

"That's my agent's client," Jayne says, knowingly.

"Olivia Potter, Katie Rose Lo, and Ruby Cole."

"Well, it's official," Amanda says, taking a big sip of lemon water from her reusable bottle. "Once I'm done with our show, I'm taking the Rose out of my name for work. Two out of the five of them had the middle name Rose? Are you kidding?"

"It is quite common for show kids," I say. It truly feels like having Rose as a middle name in show biz is about as common as having braces in the fifth grade.

"I'm Amanda Green from now on," Amanda says.

"There's that composer named Amanda Green," Jayne says through a mouth full of popcorn.

"Ugh. Yes. You're right. That's why we added the Rose to begin with," Amanda says. "Whatever. I'll have plenty of time to deal with it when I'm unemployed. Keep telling us about the auditions, Lulu. Who was the standout?"

"*I'm* torn between Penelope and Emilia," I say.

"Oh! Yay for Emilia!" Jayne says. Jayne's such a good sport.

"I feel like you just emphasized that *I'm*," Milly says. She really does have mom hearing.

"I did," I say. "*I'm* torn between Penelope and Emilia, but I feel like Pete, Susie, and Ricardo were most into Olivia. Susie liked how quickly she picked up the dance moves, Pete liked that she had her material one hundred percent memorized, and Michael had her belt up to a G and she had zero issue with it."

"Huh," Jayne says.

"They called her 'balanced.' Plus, she's exactly your size, Jayne, so they wouldn't have to make new costumes, which saves a lot of money."

"She'd wear my costumes?" Jayne has the kind of look on her face I imagine an only child might have when her parents bring home a new baby.

"Don't worry," Amanda says. "It'll be your role." She says it in a way that is so mature, so kind, it's almost heartbreaking. Amanda hasn't only grown out of her costumes during her almost year with this show. She's grown up. "Okay, someone needs to take this popcorn away from me. I can't stop."

Jayne grabs the bowl and promptly eats her feelings. "I don't think I want to hear anything else. I know I said not to leave anything out, but I changed my mind."

"Let's stop talking about it, then," Milly says. "It's almost Half Hour, anyway." Then she turns to me. "Think your brothers would like the popcorn crumbs?"

"Is Sutton Foster a true triple threat?" I reply. (Obvious hint: she is.)

"I'll take that as a yes," Milly says. "I'll run the bowl down to them and be right back."

"Wait," Amanda says. She's standing now, and has a queasy, puzzled look on her face. "I . . . I'll walk with you."

Milly looks slightly worried, but really, at this point, is there anything she can't handle? She and Amanda make their way out of the dressing room. Amanda has zero spring in her step. If anything, she's almost waddling, like she's trying to keep her legs together. Oh, theatre gods, this really is not the time for another bout of food poisoning!

"I feel like I overreacted," Jayne says.

"I don't," I say. "This whole understudy thing, it's tough on everyone. Look at Lisa and H.H. They had a . . . *moment* last week. Then when Jodie got back, she demanded to hear all about Lisa's performance."

"I know," Jayne says. "But I also know there's no point in feeling competitive or threatened. I know it's my role. Well, that it will be my role."

"Look," I say. "How you're feeling is how you're feeling." Between Amanda and Jayne, I feel like I've been validating a lot of feelings lately, but, hey, that's what friends do! "That you're aware of it is the bravest part," I say. "Just keep it all in check when the new girl gets here. Whoever she is."

"You really liked Penelope and Emilia best?" Jayne asks.

"Yeah," I say. "They also seem pretty easy to get along with."

"That's good," Jayne says. "It took us a while to get our dressing room dynamic just right; it'd be great not to have to readjust again."

"Well, we might have to," I say. "Olivia seemed nice enough, but . . ."

"But?" Jayne asks.

"I just . . . I just have a feeling," I say. "Something . . . I don't know. Maybe it was just the audition environment."

"I hope so," Jayne replies, casually falling into a split. "Because what happens backstage is just as important as what happens onstage."

Milly hurries in, popcorn bowl still in her hand. She drops the bowl on the counter and starts rummaging through her purse.

"Everything okay?" I ask. "Amanda's not sick again, is she?" I sincerely hope Amanda isn't sick again, dear reader. One, because I've seen enough friend puke for a lifetime. Two, because I want her to be able to perform all the shows she has left. And three, because I'm really not in the mood to deal with Amanda's mother.

"Should I start pin-curling my hair?" Jayne asks.

"No, no, she's doing the show," Milly says. "She's fine. I'll let her tell you herself." She finally finds what she is looking for and yanks it out of her purse. A little pink plastic package, and I know immediately what it is because a certain brother I know once used one as a bed and my mother reprimanded him for "not being considerate of the plight of human women!"

"This'll have to do for now," Milly says, almost to herself, as she hurries out the door.

"Was that a panty liner?" Jayne asks.

"Yep," I say. "I think Amanda just got her period."

Jayne and her big eyes shoot a loving glance toward the hallway. "I haven't gotten mine yet. But my sister has had hers for years. Not fun, apparently. Last month she spent an entire day at home with a heating pad on her belly."

In walks Milly, followed by Amanda, who's basically back to walking like herself but is sporting an *I'm done with surprises* look on her face.

"I've got to make a quick trip to Duane Reade," Milly says. "I'll send whoever I run into on my way downstairs up to look after you." She throws on her coat and scarf. "I trust you, of course. But it's protocol." She grabs a debit card from her wallet and hurries out.

"Well, to add to this month's theme of 'big changes,' I got my period," Amanda says.

"What does it feel like?" I ask.

"It feels funny, but I'm sure I'll get used to it. It's just part of growing up. Milly's going to buy me some pads because apparently tampons can be a little tricky at first."

"My family and I were on a trip to Spain when my sister got her period for the first time," Jayne says. "I remember her crying and saying she couldn't wait to be pregnant so she wouldn't have her period anymore."

Ummmm, I'm no expert on the matter, but I'd venture to guess being pregnant is way more intense and life changing than having a period. But . . . again, no expert.

"I guess what I'm saying is: bravo to you for being so cool about it!"

"Thanks, Jayne," Amanda says. "I'm sure it'll be a little uncomfortable when I dance, but if all the women in the ensemble can do it, then so can I. Make sure you call me when you get yours and I'll talk you through it, okay?"

"Deal," Jayne says.

Amanda smiles knowingly, like the helpful big sister she's become. "I need to warm up. Mind if I have the room?"

"Of course," I say. "We'll be outside if you need us."

Jayne sits me on her shoulder and we head out. As the door closes, I lock eyes with Amanda.

It's the surprise of the century, but here it is: I can't even express how much I'm going to miss her.

The door shuts, and I spot it—my name plaque. A sturdy rectangle with my name written in the same serifed font as the other two name plaques that have hung on the door for far longer than mine.

AMANDA ROSE GREEN
JAYNE GRIFFIN
LULU THE MOUSE

Life, I suppose, is just a series of surprises. Some more welcome than others.

THEATRE THOUGHTS with T. Mason

Lulu the Mouse. These three words are hovering over the Great White Way like a bad smell. Everyone is making such a fuss, and, in my humble opinion, it's unwarranted. Just because someone's the first to do something doesn't mean they should be doing it. This critic found the mouse's performance distracting. Unappealing. Unnecessary. Here's hoping this team of producers—and Samantha Kendall, a director who really should know better—will soon wise up and banish their token Broadway Mouse back to the basement where she belongs.

CHAPTER
ELEVEN

I F MY MOTHER WERE STILL ALIVE, SHE'D CALL THIS newspaper *spazzatura!* and she'd throw it right in the *spazzatura* where it belongs," Bet says. "After she used it to wash the windows, mind. We didn't have paper towels back then."

Usually when Bet speaks Italian, I feel happy (and hungry), but right now I just feel like *spazzatura*. (P.S. In case you haven't deduced its meaning, *spazzatura* means "garbage" in Italian.)

"I'm upset with your brother for even showing you this," my mother says. She's aggressively pulling a torn hem out of a pair of chorus boy trousers—using her teeth.

"It's not his fault," I say. "He tried to hide it and I forced him to show me." FYI, Timmy will basically read anything he can get his hands on, so please don't judge him for reading this particular publication—that shall not be named! It's already broken my heart; it doesn't get a free advertisement out of me as well.

"Look, boo," Chris says. "This little blurb is extremely nasty and uncalled for. But that's what gossip columnists get paid for." He rests a laundry basket full of undergarment ditty bags on his hip. "Being mean for a living. That's the definition of basic." Lived-longer-than-anyone-in-this-building Bet looks at Chris with a *that's not the definition of basic* look, and Chris shoots back a *you know what I mean* wink. He turns his attention back to me and, with a loving pat on the head, he says, "You'll rise above it, Lulu, like the goddess you are." Then he heads out the door to distribute clean underwear, socks, and pantyhose.

"Yes, she will!" my mother calls out. "Yes, you will," she says to me. Then she turns back to those poor trousers and sinks her teeth into the hem so hard, I'm fairly certain she's imagining the critic is actually wearing the pants.

"This particular critic has been causing trouble for decades," Bet says. "I remember when he or she wrote something cruel about Alan Alda back in the nineties. How anyone could find it in their heart to be cruel to Alan Alda, I'll never know." (Side note: Alan Alda is a grandpa-aged actor with, like, a million Emmys and is, according to Bet, "the sweetest man who ever lived." She met him when he starred in *The Apple Tree* at the Shubert in the sixties.)

"He or she?" I ask.

"T. Mason," Bet says. "Anonymous since 1988."

"More like *cowardly* since 1988," Mom scoffs, tearing out the trousers' last loose thread with the kind of simmering anger only a mother can muster.

"Indeed," Bet says. "Put this person out of your mind, Lulu. Do as young Chris said and rise above."

Rising above is often far more complicated than it

should be. But, at the very least, I have to try. Wallowing in worry never got anyone anywhere.

"Okay," I say to Bet. "I'll do my best."

———————◇———————

"Tiny, my dear, have I taught you nothing?" H.H. waltzes into her dressing room at a quarter to one, and, oh look, here I am, standing on the copy of T. "Anonymous" Mason's scathing commentary that I bribed the Hooligans to sneak up to the second floor. (The bribe included a full bowl of Milly's signature popcorn with audience-dropped Reese's Pieces sprinkled throughout, and I'm so ashamed of myself I could spit.)

H.H. unravels her cashmere scarf, removes her faux-fur earmuffs, and hangs up her coat, all while maintaining a *you know better than this, Tiny* look in my direction. Once all of her outerwear is removed and put away, she says, "We never read reviews and we never, ever read T. Mason's column."

"We read my *Times* review," I argue.

"Well," she says. "That was an article, not a review. And it practically glowed. 'Commentary' like 'Theatre Thoughts with T. Mason' is gossipy nonsense, and we should treat it as such."

"But you did read it?" I ask. (I'm so confused about the rules right now.)

"Of course I read it," H.H. says. "But only *after* I *heard* about it at Mark Fisher Fitness. And only because it concerns you and it's my job to protect you." Heather Huffman grabs the paper, then me, and makes her way to the couch-chair combo (aka the *chaise longue*, in case your French escapes you during these troubling times). "Now that the damage has already been done, what will repair things? Shall we psychoanalyze the writer? Rip up the paper? I can bring it home and use it to start a fire!" (H.H. is in possession of every New Yorker's dream, aka an apartment with a working fireplace.)

"Stop right there!" Jodie Howard squawks. "Put that down and never look at it again!"

She whirls into the room—her lashes still on from last night's show, which happens from time to time—and with a mittened hand, she snatches the paper out of H.H.'s manicured one. "This person does not deserve your time or energy. I'm throwing this madness into the alley."

She turns to head toward the windows that perch directly above Shubert Alley and I scream, "No! What if the audience reads it?!"

"Lulu is right," H.H. says, delicately plucking the paper back from Jodie like it's a stranger's snotty tissue. "Let's limit its exposure. Let us also remember not to litter."

"All right," Jodie says, tripping over her sleeping-bag-length puffy coat as she attempts to take it off. "But for heaven's sake let's get it out of this room. An evil talisman like this will haunt you for decades if you let it. Believe me—I know. I fled to Los Angeles and lived there for two traffic-filled years to escape this exact critic."

"You told me you moved there because of a 'severe vitamin D deficiency,'" H.H. says with an eyebrow raise.

"Well, yes, that too," Jodie says. "Once my D levels stabilized, I realized I couldn't let one person's negative words affect my life choices, so I sold my Nissan Altima to a script supervisor on *Frasier,* moved back to New York, and six months later I received my first Tony nomination." Someway, somehow, 90 percent of Jodie Howard's stories lead back to one or both of her Tony nominations, and, really, can you blame her?

"A lot of people read T. Mason's column, don't they?" I ask.

"While I hate to admit it, yes, they do," H.H. says. "T. Mason is frustratingly powerful."

"What if this commentary or review or whatever we're calling it . . . what if it scares off our audiences?

Or makes the producers rethink my role in the show? If T. Mason doesn't think a mouse belongs on Broadway . . . what if others agree?"

"There's no use worrying about any of it," H.H. says. "Just focus on giving a fabulous performance this afternoon, enjoying the kale and avocado salad I plan on sharing with you for dinner, then give another fabulous performance tonight."

(Side note: kale is delicious, especially when "massaged" with avocado. Try it and thank me later.)

"Precisely," Jodie Howard says. "Don't let T. Mason win."

"And!" H.H. proclaims. "Isn't Jayne's replacement arriving today?"

"She is," I say. I can't believe I let the threat of T. Mason distract me from the thing I've been excited and scared about for the last week. The new girl will be here in a half hour, if she's not here already. (If it were my first day of work, I'd be early, is all I'm saying.) Please, for the love of George and Ira Gershwin, let this new girl be easy to get along with. Because after T. Mason's meanness, anything less than kind from Olivia Potter might set me over the edge.

Oh, yes. I forgot to mention. Olivia Potter got the part.

CHAPTER
TWELVE

I T'S REALLY SURPRISING HOW SMALL IT IS BACK
here!" Olivia says. "Like, when you see a Broadway
show, you think the backstage is going to be huge
and fancy!"

Cut to me, metaphorically covering the ears of my
beloved Shubert Theatre, who needs to hear a nine-year-
old talk smack about it just as much as it needs a termite
infestation.

"It's over a hundred years old," Jayne says.

"Clearly!" Olivia says. She's examining the layers of
paint on our dressing room wall like she's a guest on one
of those home makeover shows. Then, as if a producer

has told her they need a positive comment for editing purposes, she looks at the ceiling and says, "But I like those twinkly lights."

"Thanks," Amanda says. "We put them up for my last birthday and never took them down."

"Well, please don't take them with you when you go," Olivia says. "They make the room much more fun."

Amanda squirts some eyelash glue onto her right lash, applies it to her lash line, and holds it there. With her one open eye staring straight into the mirror, she says, "The lights will stay when I go, Olivia. Don't worry."

"Fifteen Minutes, this is your Fifteen-Minute call," Pete's voice pipes from the intercom. "Fifteen Minutes, please."

"I know what Fifteen Minutes means," Olivia says. No one said she didn't, but whatever. I get wanting to seem professional on your first day. (Though this gal could chill out a tad, yes?) "It's really surprising you're not ready yet!"

Hear that phrase, dear reader. Hear: "it's really surprising." Absorb it. Memorize it. This phrase follows us around for the rest of our Saturday matinee. Everything about being backstage at a Broadway show is "really surprising!" to Olivia Potter, but not in a thrilled way. Not in an infatuated, mesmerized, awed way. But in a way that comes across as disappointed. Underwhelmed. Unimpressed.

Remember Jayne's first few days in the theatre? The way her eyes widened every time she made a new discovery? That's not what's happening with Olivia. Olivia is making it seem like the reality of my beloved Shubert Theatre home (and place of employment) doesn't live up to her dream of it.

Sure, I suppose it's possible she's purposefully trying to downplay her excitement to seem professional. Should I tell her that's *not* professional? That it's totally professional to be thrilled by every sight, sound, and set piece? That seventy-five-year-old Joe, who's in our ensemble and who has been in literally a dozen Broadway shows, is still as excited when he walks through our stage door as he was when he made his Broadway debut at the St. James back in 1967?

I'll tell her all these things and more!

But not today. We just met. I don't need to be too bossy. I need to give her a chance.

"Guess what?" Jayne says, returning from her in-between show break with a bento box from Kodama Sushi.

"What?" I ask. (To be honest, I hope it's that she doesn't want her sweet potato tempura.)

"When we left through the stage door after the show, Olivia said, 'It's really surprising more people don't wait in the alley to have autographs signed!'"

"Do you think we should say something to her?" I ask. (Yes, dear reader, I am aware that I, just moments ago, said I was going to wait to say something because I didn't want to be bossy, but . . . I take it back.)

"Say something to who?" Olivia asks. She bounds through the door, trailed by Milly. This moment is brought to you by the *Midtown turnaround*. The Midtown turn-around is the idea that you should take a peek around before you discuss something show-biz-related whilst in Midtown to make sure you don't say something you shouldn't in front of someone who shouldn't hear it.

"To . . . Milly," I say. I really do hate to lie, but it's a necessary evil sometimes. That's why some genius came up with the word "fib," lie's friendlier synonym.

"Milly, Jayne and I were talking about your wedding dress choices, and I know you love the strapless, but we really do think the one with the cap sleeves is the most you."

I follow this (true) statement with an *I'm covering up what was almost a big mess* face, and Milly, who knows me oh so well, says, "Thanks for being honest with me, Lulu. I appreciate it."

"You're getting married?" Olivia asks.

"Yes," Milly says. "In September."

"On a farm in Vermont," Jayne says.

"Are you going, Jayne?" Olivia asks hopefully.

"Sadly, Pete's not letting anyone but me take time off for my wedding," Milly says. "So the only way Jayne's going is if the show closes." The words fall out of her mouth so quickly, I'm fairly certain she doesn't even realize she's said them.

But we heard them. Boy, did we ever.

"What?" Olivia says. "My contract is until next February."

"Yes, of course," Milly says. "I don't know why I said that. Forget I said it."

"I told everyone I was working here until next February," Olivia says. It's a statement like this that makes me realize how truly inexperienced Olivia is. Sure, she can do a triple pirouette, can belt a G, can memorize lines quickly. But those things are the art of this business. The fact that a show can close long before it's supposed to? That's the business of this business.

"A lot of shows close before they're set to," Jayne

says. "Not that I've ever experienced it. This is my debut, too." She says it in a way that's so dear and so friendly—I am consistently in awe of Jayne's ability to be kind.

"We'll be fine," I say. "We're selling well! My brother Benji keeps an eye on the grosses. We made a hundred thousand dollars over our nut last week."

"Oh," Olivia says.

I can tell by the look on her face that she has no idea what I just said. Jayne can tell, too, so she, Queen of Goodness that she is, says, "What does that mean, Lulu?"

Before I can say anything, a ball of gray whirls in like Dorothy's twister and says, "A show's nut is basically the amount it costs to run." I have no idea how long my brother has been lingering outside our door, listening to our conversation, eyeing Jayne's uneaten tempura, but I promise you, dear reader, I will find out. It's so not okay to snoop on people. Though I won't shame him in front of Olivia. He is my favorite brother, after all. (Don't tell the others. Thanks.)

"Olivia, meet my brother Benji," I say. "Benji, meet Olivia."

"It's a pleasure," Benji replies with a crooked smile I'm sure he thinks seems charming and not creepy. He's dropped his Benji the British Butler accent in exchange for the suave speak of Max Bialystock. (See: *The Producers*— and really, do see it, it's a fabulous show.) A fast-talking, no-nonsense, New Yorker-y kind of accent. "As I was sayin', a show's nut is what it costs to run. The grosses are how much money a show makes before the running costs are taken out. Lately, thanks to my sister's history-making star turn, our grosses are greater than our running costs, resulting in a profit, also known as our 'net.'" He looks at me and smiles a slick Golden Age of Broadway smile, but underneath it, there's my proud brother, and maybe I won't reprimand him later for having snooped on us.

"I see," Olivia says. "It's surprising you know so much about all this."

This is Benji's first "it's surprising" of the day, so I'm

guessing he doesn't want to scream right now. (But I sure do!)

"It's surprising most actors don't know the half of it," Benji says. "Show business is a business, after all. It's important to understand how your bread gets buttered."

"Very true," Milly says, stifling a little laugh. Watching my hairy brother explain the financial ins and outs of show business is understandably amusing to a grown-up, though from the look on Milly's face, she finds it absolutely adorable. "Perhaps we'll enlist Benji for a Business of Show Business tutorial sometime. But let's put a pin in it for now. Amanda will be back from dinner any minute and she'll need to start getting ready."

"Any questions," Benji says, "you know where to find me."

"Thanks, Benji," Jayne says. "You're so smart."

If he had a top hat, this would be the moment he'd tip it, creating a really solid visual button for this scene. But, instead, he just scurries off in a whirl of hormones, shedding his Mr. Producer *savoir faire* for his true identity: boy who crushes on every girl he meets.

"Your brother's the best," Jayne says. "That was really useful information."

"I like singing and dancing, my brother likes crunching numbers," I say. "Genetics are weird."

"I'm an only child," Olivia says.

"Me too," Amanda says. As she crosses the doorway into the dressing room, a waft of sweetness arrives with her. "Seems we have a lot in common, Olivia." She pulls a box out of a bag, revealing the source of the most delicious smell I've smelled since the arrival of Jayne's bento box. "Surprise! Schmackary's for all! Have you had them before, Olivia?"

Let's stop everything for a moment so we can immerse ourselves in the wonder that is Schmackary's. Though I've never been to the actual store (because it's on Forty-Fifth just east of Ninth Avenue and, as you know, I've never been off Forty-Fourth Street), I can easily explain their menu because their menu consists of cookies. All kinds of cookies. From classic chocolate chip to maple bacon, and they're all heavenly. Only a mere two months ago, Amanda pulled a warm snickerdoodle out of a bag and didn't even offer me a crumb. Now, here she is with a half dozen to share with everyone, including me. Change is possible, Team. Change is possible.

"Of course I know Schmackary's," Olivia says. "I take theatre jazz at Broadway Dance. It's on the same street."

You and I both know that Amanda has the power to snap back at Olivia with a retort so nasty and hurtful, Olivia would most likely hide under our dressing room counter for the rest of the show. But, instead, Amanda says, "Well, then, you get first pick. Since I'm sure you have a favorite."

Milly smiles proudly and says, "That's very nice of you, Amanda. Go ahead, Olivia."

This gesture—this kindness—softens Olivia. I've

noticed, dear reader, that repeated acts of kindness can wear anyone down, just as water has the power to wear away stone.

Olivia smiles simply and says, "I'll take the s'mores cookie, if that's all right."

"Absolutely," Amanda says.

Olivia removes the marshmallowy goodness from the box. Jayne takes a classic chocolate chip, and Milly goes for an oatmeal scotchie. (Am I drooling? I think I'm drooling. Yep, that's drool.)

"I'll take the cookies and cream," Amanda says. "I know peanut butter cup is your favorite." Amanda kneels down so I can peer into the box.

"You are correct, my friend. Thanks." She plops the cookie down in front of me, and if you think it'll take me longer to eat this cookie than it'll take the other girls, I'm here to tell you you're wrong.

"Two more cookies left," Amanda says. "I guess we'll have to split them during intermission!"

"Does this happen every Saturday?" Olivia asks. (Proud of her for admitting she doesn't know something. Let's hear it for progress, people!)

"Nope," Amanda says. "This is a 'Welcome to Broadway' treat, from me to you. I hope you love it here as much as I have." She chokes up a bit on the word *love,* which immediately triggers the beginnings of tears from me, Jayne, and Milly. (I don't expect Olivia to cry. She met Amanda five hours ago.)

"You still have ten shows left," I say. "Are we going to cry during all of them?"

"Probably," Milly says, popping a bite of oatmeal scotchie into her mouth.

"We've got to stop now, though," Jayne says. "Amanda needs to get ready for the show."

"My second-to-last Saturday night on Broadway," Amanda sighs. "On second thought, I'm going to need an entire cookie to myself at intermission."

"Go for it," Jayne says, passing her a tissue.

"I get a cookie, and in a little over a week, you get a role," Amanda says. "And that's just the way the cookie crumbles."

We all—even Olivia—look at Amanda and burst out laughing.

"I had to say it!" Amanda says. "It was too perfect!"

"We'd expect nothing less from Broadway's Amanda Rose Green," I say. "Who you will always, always be. No one can take that away from you."

Amanda pops her shoulder, tucks her chin, and, like a coy cabaret singer, begins to sing the Gershwins' "They Can't Take That Away from Me." (You probably know it from the musical *Crazy for You* and its brilliant original Broadway cast recording, but the song was actually written for Fred Astaire for an old movie called *Shall We Dance*.)

After a few bars, we all join in, because that's just how we do things here on Broadway, here as friends. No matter where we are or where we go, we will always know the lyrics.

Eight days later, Amanda and I are in the wings, waiting for our trombone-slide cue to enter for bows. I spy the first round of chorus members run on for their bows, so that means we've got less than a minute until we get to ours. Less than a minute until Amanda's final bow of her Broadway debut.

Amanda lifts me up in her cupped palms so we're face-to-face. Milly's prediction came true: we spent the majority of the last week crying, and this moment is no different.

"I'm sorry for everything before Jayne's debut," Amanda says, tears pooling in her eyes.

"Don't be," I say. I can feel the tears brimming up inside of me, like waves prepping for a crash. "It all happened the way it was supposed to."

"I was so mean," Amanda says. "So mean."

"You were afraid," I say.

"I was afraid of this moment," Amanda says. "I don't want this to be over."

I channel my mother and say, "This is only the beginning, Amanda."

"I hope so," she says.

"I know so," I say.

She's crying so hard right now, I'm not really sure how she's going to make it through bows. But there's the trombone slide, so whether we're ready or not, it's time for our last bow together.

And then, faster than you can say "Merrily We Roll Along," we're onstage and the audience is applauding. I look to stage left and see Milly and Jayne and Olivia standing in the wings, all three of them crying and applauding. (Olivia's tears are a little less hiccupy than Jayne's and Milly's, but, again, I get that. She's known Amanda for a week.) Pete, Susie, and Ricardo are next to them, clapping and hollering. Rosa has snuck away from her post at the stage door. I hear Dan's and Artie's distinctive New York yells booming down from the fly floor. My dad and brothers are huddled offstage right, and next to them are my mom and Bet. And next to them are Jeremiah and Chris and the rest of the hair and wardrobe departments.

And our cast. Our beautiful, kind, talented cast. They are clapping and cheering like I've never seen before. It's as if, right in this very moment, they're sewing together a patchwork of memories and love and support that will soon be ready to be wrapped around Amanda. So she can take us with her. So she'll never have to be alone. So she'll never have to be afraid again.

H.H. plops me into her pocket for our company bow, and as we all begin to walk backward upstage like we always do, to make room for the curtain to descend, Stella takes Amanda by the hand—which prompts H.H. to take me out of her pocket and sit me on her shoulder—and Stella walks downstage center with Amanda. If anything can brighten my spirits, it's an unscripted moment from two-time Tony winner Stella James.

"Hello, everyone," Stella calls out to the audience. "If you may permit us a few more moments of your time." Our cast has followed Stella's lead and has formed a bit of a half-oval around Amanda. This is the first time we're saying goodbye to an onstage cast member. We said goodbye to Maya earlier in the winter, but because she didn't perform on the night of her departure, there was no possibility of an onstage goodbye. Come to think of it, I've seen five shows come and go here at the Shubert, and I've seen cast members leave each show, and yet I've never experienced a moment like this. Then again, I've never known a leading lady like Stella James.

"Tonight, you were lucky enough to witness the final performance of Amanda Rose Green," Stella begins. The audience murmurs and *awwwws*. (Amanda's mother, who's sitting fourth row on the aisle, emits an exasperated, "UGHHHH.")

"Her final performance in this show, at least. For I have no doubt this is the first of many Broadway appearances for our Amanda."

Our Amanda. I see the words land on her. I see her brain register that in addition to repaired relationships with the gals in our dressing room, she has also repaired a relationship with Stella. With the whole company. She began her journey here as a stuffy, combative, scared little girl. She leaves us today a young lady who knows it's okay to be vulnerable and imperfect, who knows how lucky she is to have had this experience, who knows the importance of being a team player. This debut was more than just theatre, this debut set the foundation for the rest of her life.

"So, if you'd be so kind as to sing along with us as we bid happy trails to Amanda Rose Green."

On cue—no, really, I'm pretty sure they rehearsed this while I wasn't looking—Susie strides out with a dozen long-stemmed yellow roses and hands them to Amanda.

(It just hit me that yellow roses represent friendship, and if that isn't a classy purchase, I don't know what is.) Through the roses, Amanda hugs Susie around her waist. Sure, Amanda's grown a few inches while she's been here, but Susie's legs might as well be ten feet long.

Stella nods to our conductor, Michael, in the pit, who cues the orchestra, and she begins to sing.

After a bar or two, the rest of the company joins in.

Followed by the entire audience.

All one thousand fourteen people. (Benji makes it a point to find out the audience count for each performance.)

We all sing to our Amanda. And she sings along, too, through her tears, because she's Broadway's Amanda Rose Green, and always will be.

THEATRE THOUGHTS with T. Mason

My sources at the Shubert tell me leading lady Stella James is secretly not so happy about one of her current costars. No, I'm not talking about Jayne Griffin, who recently replaced original cast member Amanda Rose Green. (Miss Green had grown too tall for the role, so her contract was not renewed. Though I hear bad behavior might have been a contributing factor as well.) No, I'm not talking about Miss Griffin, who is lovely in her Broadway debut. The costar to whom I refer is a mouse. I'm told Stella refuses to interact with Lulu (the mouse) when she's not onstage, and that she's furious with the producers for allowing this publicity stunt to continue. Apparently, she's worried about her and the rest of the company's health. Let's not forget that mice carry and spread disease. . . . I must say, I share Ms. James's concerns wholeheartedly.

CHAPTER
THIRTEEN

HELLO, LITTLE ONE," STELLA SAYS. I'M IN MY
basement nest, curled atop a booklet of fabric
samples (courtesy of Jodie Howard's apartment renovation), like the princess and the pea. The top
layer is some sort of faux suede that's doing an excellent
job absorbing my tears.

"May I come in?"

"Of course," I say. Though I don't jump up like I
usually do when I see Stella James. I don't stand straight,
eager, ready to sing a duet or help her run lines. I stay
curled up. Because I'm bluer than a sapphire right
now, Team.

"I'd like to discuss T. Mason's latest column," Stella says. She sits down next to me, cross-legged in black yoga pants and a soft cotton turtleneck. On top of it all, she's sporting a sweater-robe hybrid and it's all so chic I almost feel better, but then . . . I don't. "You know nothing she wrote is true, right?"

"Jayne is lovely in her role," I say.

"Well, yes, that is true," Stella says. "I meant the part about you and me."

I see my mom and dad lingering at the entrance to my nest. Mom's holding a bottle cap full of hot chocolate and Dad's got a huge piece of—hold on, lemme smell it—Wisconsin cheddar.

"I absolutely adore you, and have since the moment we met," Stella says. "Watching you make your Broadway debut has been one of the high points of my career. Of my life, actually."

"Really?" I ask.

"Really," she says. "And that part about me being

scared for my health? It's a bold-faced lie."

"I've never gotten you sick, and I never would," I say. "I'm really clean."

"Of course you are," Stella says. "I will always stand up for you. Always."

"Thanks, Stella," I say. "I knew deep down T. Mason wasn't telling the truth, but even lies can hurt sometimes."

"Yes, they can," Stella says. "And I'm telling you right now, if one more untrue word is written about you, I'm doing something about it."

"That's very nice of you," my mother interjects. She makes her way toward me, not spilling one drop of precious hot chocolate. "But we don't want to cause any trouble."

"For Lulu or for the show," my dad says. (Last night, when my dad read T. Mason's column, he got so upset he ate six Milano cookies plus two paper wrappers.)

"T. Mason—whoever he or she is—has gotten away with too much for far too long. One more mention of our Lulu and this Tony winner is getting involved," Stella says.

She winks at me when she says Tony winner, because she knows I call her Tony winner Stella James like it's her full name. (If I ever won a Tony, I would legally change my name to Tony Winner Lucy Louise "Lulu" the Broadway Mouse—if we mice actually had paperwork for that sort of thing.)

"Now," she says. "Chin up, young lady. It's Friday night on Broadway and we have a show to do."

CHAPTER
FOURTEEN

I . Have. News." Jodie Howard staccatos her way into her and H.H.'s dressing room. She's ditched her full-length sleeping bag coat for a short puffy jacket that has *Apartment, The Pilot* embroidered on the sleeve. (If I were a TV producer of a pilot that was hoping to get picked up to series, I can't say that I would waste money on winter-spring transitional jackets for my entire cast and crew. But apparently there's a lot of money in TV, so . . . I'll zip my theatre-mouse lip.)

"*Apartment* got picked up?" H.H. asks.

"We haven't heard yet," Jodie says. "We won't know officially until later in the spring. BUT. In the meantime

. . . I got another job!"

H.H. looks as though she's on a first date and she just realized she forgot to put on deodorant. In truth, though, the look on her face is courtesy of a bit of envy mixed with a whole lot of not wanting to deal with Lisa Logan. Plus, H.H. just isn't H.H. when her Jodie Howard's out of the building.

"What's the job?" H.H. asks.

"Two days on a movie with—wait for it—"

I can tell from the shift in H.H.'s expression that it doesn't matter who the heck Jodie is working with on a movie; H.H. is relieved it's only two days.

"TOM HANKS!" Jodie shrieks. "Can you believe it?"

"Wow!" I say, handing H.H. a bobby pin so she can complete pin curl number six.

"I'm over the moon. I play a saleswoman at Saks Fifth Avenue. Tom comes in to buy a sweater set for his lady friend—it's a *hilarious* scene but also a bit sad. *Layered.*"

H.H. smiles and curls a section of hair around her

finger. "That's wonderful, Jodie, truly wonderful." I can tell she's holding something back, but Jodie, bless her, doesn't clock H.H.'s vibe. She's excited about Tom Hanks, and rightfully so. He's "charming and talented, but in a really approachable way." (Direct quote, my mother.) If someone made a cartoon movie about my life and cast humans to voice the characters, I'd want Tom Hanks to voice my dad. He's the perfect combination of funny, loving, and not to be messed with.

"Guess who else got a role in a movie?" I say. (Hint: it isn't me. Rome wasn't built in a day, Team.)

"Who?" Jodie asks, a smidge of jealousy sneaking out of her like my brothers sneak into the lower lobby during the second act to forage for candy.

"Jayne!" I say.

"Well isn't that wonderful," H.H. says. She's done with her pin curls now, so she pulls her wig cap over her head and secures it with one, two, three, four, five pointy bobby pins.

"She's playing Meryl Streep's granddaughter," I say.

Now it's Jodie's turn to attempt to stifle her envy. "*Meryl* STREEP?" she says.

I think this is the card game equivalent of someone throwing down a pair of kings, thinking they'll win the game with ease, only to have the next player throw down two aces. No offense to Tom Hanks, but there's a whole song about Meryl Streep in the stage musical version of *Fame*. It doesn't get much bigger than that, am I right?

"That's quite the film debut," H.H. says. She pulls out her pillbox with the days of the week on it, opens up Tuesday and pops three vitamins, which, combined, are half my size, and chases them with some coconut water. (She's been on a major health kick since her seventeenth annual thirty-fifth birthday.)

"It really is," Jodie says. "I'm *thrilled* for her. Now if you'll pardon me for a few minutes I'm going to run down to stage management to request the days off for my movie. Not to be insensitive, but I want to make sure my work days don't conflict with Jayne's." Jodie Howard hurries out of the room to claim her days on our company calendar. Technically, two principals can't take personal days at the same time, hence the hustle.

"Pete would let them both go," H.H. says. "We're far enough into our run for those silly rules to not mean as much."

"She's just excited, I guess," I say. "I sure would be."

"I would be, too," H.H. says. She's looking at herself in the mirror like she doesn't recognize the reflection staring back at her. It's not sadness as much as confusion and disappointment.

"Everything okay?" I ask. She may be a grown-up, but she's my human grown-up best friend, and when my human grown-up best friend looks confused and disappointed, it's my job to know the cause.

"I auditioned for the role Jodie got," H.H. says. "I hadn't had a film audition in almost a year, and I went in and I felt so good about it. I was certain I booked it. So naive."

"That's not naive," I say. "That's hopeful. You have to be hopeful."

"I have to be realistic," H.H. says. "I'm thankful for my theatre career, I really am. I can pay my bills, I have great health insurance, I can afford the occasional trip to Bermuda. But I really thought that by this age I would be even further along. I thought by this age that I'd be Jodie."

Yes, Team, I'm aware that the human adult who taught me about the difference between jealousy and envy is now admitting that she's jealous of her adult human best friend. Adults aren't perfect; they're learning and growing and hurting just like we are, and sometimes we need to be there for them just like they are for us.

"I'm sorry," I say. "I know something will click soon."

"I don't know that something will click soon," H.H.

says. "I fear that the path I thought my life was headed down now has a tree across it, and I'm too old to move it."

"Excellent metaphor," I say, because I don't know what else to say.

"Thank you, Tiny," H.H. says. "Thank you for being my tiny friend, and for sticking by me even when I'm acting jealous and ridiculous."

"Anytime," I say. "And you know what? There was a giant tree across my path, too. And I had pretty much given up on being able to move it. And then one day I got distracted by a friend who needed me, and helping that friend was the equivalent of realizing I could just *grand jeté* right over that tree."

"Beautifully said," H.H. replies, love in her eyes.

"Meh, it could use some work," I say. "When I have Timmy write my biography, I'll have to tighten up that metaphor." I pick up her tube of eyelash glue and walk it over to her. She removes the cap, lines a faux lash up to the tip of the glue, and I gently squirt just the right amount of glue onto the edge of the lash.

I realize, in this moment, that I love this backstage routine as much as I love performing onstage. That being an actor is just as much an offstage experience as it is an onstage one. That one day, hopefully not in the near future, this exact routine will no longer exist. H.H. will be at home in front of her fireplace or working at the Ambassador Theatre over on Forty-Ninth Street or at a regional theatre somewhere far away from here. My story will continue long after this company leaves my house. It's an idea that both terrifies and intrigues me. The idea of what's next.

Will the next show's cast be as welcoming as our current cast? Will I perform in other shows—maybe even at other theatres? Will *I* be in a movie with Tom Hanks and/or Meryl Streep? Or will I be sent "back to the basement" to mend hems, sew on buttons, and clean the clothes of the humans who get to sing and dance like I used to?

Who knows what the future will bring? Whatever happens, I'll find a way to deal with it, good or bad or in between. But for now, we're here. It's a Tuesday in early March, and we have a show to do. And although a part of H.H. wishes she were working in front of the camera, on something new, even just for a day or two, I can't tell you how happy I am to be here with her right now.

"No offense to Timothy because, as you know, I absolutely adore our little bookworm," H.H. says, taking the lash and placing it on her lash line, her mouth ajar a bit like it always is when she applies a lash or puts eyedrops in her eyes, "but when the time comes to write your story, I have a feeling you'll be writing it yourself."

"I'm not a writer," I say. "I'm an actress."

"You can be both," H.H. says. "No rule against that. You'll get yourself a vintage typewriter, because you're elegant like that, and you'll tap, tap, tap away on its keys like you're Fred and Ginger." (She's referring to Fred Astaire and Ginger Rogers, legendary dance partners who performed in many films together, including *Shall We Dance,* which I mentioned earlier.)

"We'll see," I say. "For now, I'm happy with where I am. Ecstatic with where and who I am."

"You know what," H.H. says. "After a brief moment of panic and reflection, so am I."

"Half Hour, this is your Half-Hour call," Pete's voice croons through the intercom. "Half Hour, please. Half Hour."

CHAPTER
FIFTEEN

I T'S HALF HOUR," OLIVIA SAYS. "WHERE'S JERE-
miah?!"

"He'll be here at Five Minutes to Places," Milly
says. This is the third time she's said this, because it's the
third time Olivia has asked.

"It's just really surprising that Jayne doesn't get her
wig on earlier. What if something goes wrong?"

"Nothing's gone wrong so far," I say. This being
Olivia's first performance, I thought I'd better stick with
her for her entire preshow; H.H. agreed. Now I'm sort of
regretting my decision . . .

"Don't jinx me, Lulu!" Olivia snaps.

"Lulu is right," Milly says. "I know this is new for you, but it's routine for everyone else. We're here for you. I promise, there's enough time for everything. More than enough time."

More than enough time is right, seeing as aside from her wig, Olivia is completely ready. She's already warmed up her body and her voice, her makeup is *heavily* on, her hair is pin-curled, and she's in her undergarments, tights, and robe. She tried to put on her vanilla velvet opening-scene dress, but Milly put a stop to it for fear something really would go wrong. You know how much blush and Throat Coat tea could accidentally be spilled on a vanilla velvet dress in the span of a half hour? Enough to create a whole lot of last-minute work for my mom, that's how much.

"I feel like not enough attention was given to my put-in," Olivia says. *At least you had a put-in*, I'd like to remind her. (And did remind her, when it was held last week and she said the same thing. Oh. I should probably remind you, dear reader: a "put-in" is a dress rehearsal run-through for understudies or new cast members, so they can perform the whole show once, all the way through, before they get up in front of a live, paying audience.)

You know who didn't have a put-in? Me. Or Jayne. And we both did just fine without one. Well . . . okay, sure, I suppose there was that little hiccup with Jayne being struck by stage fright and me making my Broadway debut while helping her out of it, but . . . that all worked out beautifully in the end!

"Olivia," Milly says. "Your put-in was given plenty of attention. Even Stella was there. She's never at put-ins."

It's true. Usually Stella's understudy, Mindy, plays her part during all rehearsals and put-ins. But Stella—probably sensing Olivia's . . . intensity, let's call it—decided it would be best to be there. It was a smooth-sailing put-in, just like it'll be a smooth-sailing performance.

"Should we do a brief meditation?" I ask. "I can teach you how. I'm really learning a lot at between-shows yoga on Wednesdays."

"I know how to meditate, Lulu, don't be silly!" Olivia snips. "I'm fine. I'm just ready for the show to start."

"Me too," I say. I look at Milly and she nods in silent agreement.

A Places call for this performance really can't come soon enough. This gal is stressing me out.

OMMMMMMMMMM.

———————◇———————

TWO DAYS AND THREE SHOWS LATER, JAYNE AND I ARE sitting in my nest, a place where we're sure Olivia won't find us, because she's never even asked where I live.

"Well?" Jayne asks. "How was she?"

"Tell me about Meryl Streep first!" I say.

"You know me better than to think you can distract me like that," Jayne says. "Spill."

I sigh. "She was great." It's not a matter of opinion, dear reader. Olivia was great in Jayne's role. Which, of course, makes sense, since she was hired to play the role. (This is why you should never be upset when you see that an understudy is on. They're usually just as qualified to play the part as the person who always plays the part.)

"Oh," Jayne says. "Well, good for her. I'm glad. I'm glad everything went well."

"It's okay to feel funny about it," I say.

"It feels like . . . like I left for summer camp and came back to find my dog likes my brother better than me," Jayne says. "Does that make sense?"

"It does," I say. "But remember what happened when you went on for Amanda. Two shows later, you were back in the dressing room doing homework. And the same thing will happen to Olivia today. It's still your part."

"For now," Jayne says. "Don't forget what happened a week after I went on."

"Olivia isn't going to get your part," I say.

"I know," Jayne says. "Logically, I know that. But I still feel funny."

"Then feel funny," I say. "I'm here for it!" I do a high kick—a high kick that's getting higher and higher as the weeks go on—and this makes Jayne smile.

"Let's feel funny together for the next ten minutes and then forget all about it," Jayne says. "Because I'm sure Olivia will be sad today. It's hard going back to no makeup, regular clothes, and homework in the dressing room. I remember that feeling too."

"My dad heard someone in the box office say I was just as good in the role as you are," Olivia reports. She's on the floor doing math homework, and this (super inappropriate) comment falls out of her mouth just as easily as adding two and two to make four.

"Well," Jayne says, "that's why you got the job, isn't it? I'm so glad the three shows went so well, Olivia."

What. A. Saint. On. Earth.

Olivia looks a bit thrown, like she was expecting

one response and got another. There really isn't anything else she can say to (dear, kind, evolved) Jayne, other than, "Thanks."

I'm sitting on Milly's lap and I can actually feel her body relax. I, too, am glad that this comment didn't lead to a whole big thing. Because I already have too much on my mind.

Our ticket sales have dropped.

Dramatically. Drastically. Depressingly.

The drop in sales directly correlates with T. Mason's latest column; it's hard to believe audiences would buy that Stella doesn't like working with me, or that I'm . . . dangerous. But I guess they do. If Stella doesn't like me, they shouldn't like me; if she's afraid of me, then they should be afraid of me, is what I'm saying they're thinking. I can't see any other reason why our sales would drop so much, and so fast. Why is it that humans always seem to let bad things influence them more than good?

I haven't told the girls. I don't want to freak them out. So I'm just telling you. I'm telling you what Benji told me: "We haven't made our nut for four weeks straight."

As I sit here and watch Jayne put on her makeup, Milly knit, and Olivia do her homework—in an understandingly grumpy way—I can't help but wonder if it's time for me to metaphorically go back to my homework, too. If it's time for me to give the role back to Teddy the Bear. Teddy the Bear who T. Mason never made a peep about. Teddy the Bear who is stuffed, who doesn't sing along, who blends in.

I got my dream. Maybe it's time I give it back.

CHAPTER
SIXTEEN

I F I WERE RUNNING THINGS, I WOULDN'T CALL A company meeting just to fire you, Lulu." Benji is sitting serenely on a kitchen sponge that Bet gifted us for Christmas—"to ensure an extra cozy winter"— and I'm pacing around our living room so repetitively that I'm worried I might wear a hole in our concrete floor. "This company meeting isn't about you. I'm sure of it."

"What if they're calling the whole company together so they can all, as a group, convince me to quit?" If I didn't need my nails for things like climbing, I'd be biting them down to the skin right now. (Gross. So sorry.)

"Lulu. Listen to yourself." This from Walt over in the corner, spread out on some worn-out washcloths.

Next to him, Matty is halfway into a peanut M&M's bag, sucking up every last crumb. From inside the bag, he mumbles, "You're being ridiculous, sis."

"Am I? Am I?" I'm one "Am I?" away from spinning out of control.

"Should I recite it again?" Timmy asks. Although he knew better than to remove the posting from the call board, that didn't stop my reads-a-page-a-minute brother from memorizing what it said.

"Yes," I say. "Maybe we missed a clue."

Timmy grabs a paper clip from his office supply collection, stands up, and puts the paper clip up to his mouth like it's a microphone. I appreciate that he's trying to make this fun, but we're literally dealing with my future here, so . . .

"Attention, Company. Tuesday at 5:00 p.m. there will be a company meeting in the house. All cast and crew are required to attend. Following the meeting, Actors' Equity members will then be released until our 6:30 Half-Hour call. Thank you, Management (on behalf of the Producers)."

"Very straightforward," Benji says. "It's a company meeting. It could be anything. They could be bringing in a movie star to replace Stella."

"Oh, please," I say.

"What?" Benji says. "Happens all the time. A nice eight-week break for Stella, premium ticket pricing and sold-out houses for us. It's a win-win."

"Do you think it's about Jayne?" Walt asks. "Maybe they're replacing her with Olivia. She was really good." Walt is gnawing on a pistachio like humans gnaw on an ear of corn. He's such an animal.

"First of all," Benji says, "Olivia gave three great shows, but she's no Jayne. Second of all, Jayne is under contract. She's not going anywhere."

"Then it has to be about me," I say. "Ticket sales have dropped so much since I started."

"Not true," Timmy says. "Ticket sales rose when you first made your debut. I read about it on Playbill.com."

"You also heard about it from your brother, but whatever," Benji says.

"And then they fell again," I say. "After T. Mason wrote that first column. About *my debut*. The sales fell and they fell hard. It's me. They're going to ask me to go. I'm a novelty that's no longer novel. A jewel that's lost its sparkle. This experiment of a mouse on Broadway is over. I know it."

My dad walks in, returning home from whatever he does for work. "You know what they say in baseball, Lulu?"

"You know I don't know what they say, Dad." He knows this.

"They say 'It ain't over 'til it's over.'" The answer comes from Jayne, as she appears at the entrance to our living room.

"That's exactly right," my dad says. "You can worry all you want, but until the last pitch of the last inning, you won't know the outcome of the game."

"Maybe we won't strike out like we think we will," Jayne says. "Maybe we'll hit a home run and go into extra innings."

Bless Jayne for going along with this sports metaphor and for trying to be so optimistic, even though I can tell by the look on her face, and the way she can't stand still, that she's just as scared as I am. But she shouldn't be. Benji's right: she's under contract. Her job is safe. I'm the one with no paperwork. No union or agent to protect me. I'm the first mouse to ever perform on Broadway, and I'm certain Broadway's first-ever anonymous theatre critic is about to take my dream away from me, all without ever revealing his or her face.

But instead of saying all this out loud, I just look at Jayne and my dad and say, "It ain't over 'til it's over." Then I nod. Because though I might be minutes away from losing my job, I will never, ever pass up the opportunity for a solid button. I am Lulu the Broadway Mouse, and I always, always will be.

IT'S FIVE O'CLOCK. 5:02, TO BE EXACT. MILLY'S HANDS are resting on her lap and I'm seated atop her left thigh. With each *tick . . . tick . . . tick . . .* of her watch, I feel the knots in my stomach twist and swirl, and it's moments like these that make me thankful I'm a tiny mouse, because if I puke underneath the seats no one will notice.

The whole company is gathered in the house. Aside from tech rehearsal and occasional return visits from our director, Samantha, who likes to hold notes sessions in the house, we've never all sat out here together. (Notes sessions, by the way, are just what they sound like: an hour or so when Samantha gives notes on the show, how it's holding up, things actors could change or focus on to make the show even stronger, that sort of thing.)

It should feel comforting, being here with all of my favorite humans, but I am currently the opposite of comforted. And I think I can safely say the same about everyone else; you can practically smell the tension and anxiety in the air. We're all being as close to silent as possible—though the occasional whispered "I'm so nervous" or "What could it be?" flutters around the room like a fly that won't quit.

Finally, at 5:03, Pete and Ricardo walk out onstage, followed by our lead producers. Three humans—two women and one man—who hold my future in their hands.

Pete and I lock eyes for a split second before he looks away and down at his feet.

He can't even look at me. That's how bad this is. It's me. I know it's me.

A little hand scoops me up and puts me in her lap. I can feel Jayne's heart beating in her stomach. "Whatever happens," she whispers, "I've got you and you've got me."

I look over at Stella. She has quite the poker face, I'll tell you that. I have absolutely no idea what she's thinking. What if they do replace her with Viola Davis or Emily Blunt or some other fabulous, stage-worthy celebrity?

Will she be relieved? Will she be jealous? What if Stella cries? I've never seen Stella cry. What if—

"We've called you all here today because we have some not-so-great news," Female Producer with Glasses says.

"As I'm sure you've noticed," Lone Male Producer says, "our audiences have been quite light lately, just as they were for most of January and a good portion of the fall. There are many factors at play. Weather, timing, press—"

"While we are proud of this show, it is an expensive one to run," Female Producer with Bangs says.

I look around the house. I can see the wheels turning in my castmates' heads. I can see flashes of realization pass over their faces—a lot of them have heard speeches like this before because a lot of them have been in other Broadway shows.

Suddenly, I know.

It's not me. Not *just* me.

"We're very sorry to tell you that our dear show will play its last Broadway performance on May first."

We're closing.

It's so much bigger than me.

But no matter what anyone tells me, I know it's my fault.

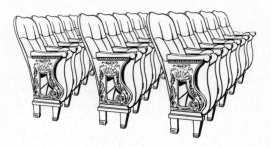

CHAPTER
SEVENTEEN

NEEDLESS TO SAY, TUESDAY'S SHOW IS WONKY. After Female Producer with Bangs uttered the fateful words *May first,* we all immediately burst into tears. Truly, everyone. From Olivia, our youngest cast member, to Joe, our oldest, and everyone in between. We all cried and held each other. We had been told that in one month we'd no longer see our family every day, we'd no longer get to dance these dances and sing these songs eight times a week, those of us receiving paychecks would have to do without soon; our reactions were justified.

While we all continued to cry and blubber, Stella walked up onstage via the stage left pass door. (You know those doors to the right and left of the stage? Those are called pass doors. I may be devastated, but I will continue to keep you in the know about theatre terms, dear reader. Also, *never* try to go through those doors if you're an audience member. You'll be stopped faster than you can say "Just because you see an outlet up onstage doesn't mean you can charge your phone in it.")

For a moment I thought Stella was going to give a speech, but instead she approached the producers, they said a few words that we couldn't hear, and then they all followed her offstage left, presumably to chat in her dressing room.

And the rest of us? Well, we continued to cry. And conjecture. And vent our anger and frustration and disappointment. Harper sniffled and said, "Well, I guess I'll go to that *Miss Saigon* tour audition," while Jodie hiccupped out, "*Apartment* had better get picked up, is all I can say," and loudly blew her nose into an already snotty tissue.

We pulled ourselves together enough to do our show,

of course. I doubt the audience could sense anything was wrong, but the moment someone would make an exit, they'd be teary and blue again. Each note, each dance move, each bow—they all felt more important than ever before because in the blink of an eye, they were no longer endless. They had an expiration date. Sunday, May first— end scene, curtains, that's a wrap, folks.

It's after the show now and we're back in our dressing room. Jayne has pulled out her final pin curl, and her hair is bouncy and glamorous. Maybe this Meryl Streep film will make her a movie star; she certainly looks the part.

"I'll tell your parents, girls," Milly says. "If Pete hasn't called them already."

"We rented an apartment," Olivia huffs. It's the fifth time she's told us this since we received our closing notice a mere five hours ago, and I'll tell ya, it's all I can do to not look her straight in the eye and say, "You only live an hour away from the theatre. Renting an apartment was an unnecessary, silly thing to do. You jinxed us. This is all your fault, Olivia. You and your impulsive parents." But I keep my mouth shut, of course, because, one, I'm not mean, and, two, this isn't Olivia's fault. Because, three, it's my fault.

"You don't worry about that," Milly says. "Your parents will figure it out." She pulls her coat off its hanger, turns to me and says, "Will you be okay?"

"Not tonight," I say. "But eventually, I suppose." There are times in life when an actress can be dramatic offstage, and tonight's one of those times.

"Knock, knock," H.H. says from the doorway. "How's everyone doing?"

"We're sad," Jayne says.

"Of course you are," H.H. says. "I'm sad, too."

"My family rented an apartment," Olivia says.

"Well, that was a silly thing to do," H.H. replies. I can always trust my H.H. to speak the truth I'm too nice to say. "I'm here to escort you down to your nest, Tiny."

"Thanks," I say. She pops me into her bag, and I grip

onto its edge so I can see what's in front of me: Milly, Olivia, and Jayne are shuffling down our rubber-coated nonslip stairs like they're a bunch of four-day-old balloons that are just about spent. Usually, we girls are peppy on Tuesdays because we're rested from our Monday day off and we're excited about our two-show day tomorrow. But not tonight. Tonight, we're deflated.

Rosa's at her post at the stage door, half-watching the end of one of those *Chicago* shows on NBC. (No, not the musical. Don't get excited.)

"I'm very sorry this is happening, girls," she says. "Of all the casts who have walked through this door, this cast is my favorite."

"Mine, too," I say. And not just because this cast helped me make my Broadway debut, but because this cast is the first one that's truly seen me, understood me, and appreciated me.

Olivia and Jayne don't say anything—probably because any words that fall out of their mouths will come with tears to match. They just give Rosa hugs good night and head out into Shubert Alley.

As they exit through the stage door, Stella enters through it. "Thought I'd get my signing done early tonight so I could have a little chat with you, Lulu," Stella says. "Shall we go downstairs?"

"Sure," I say. She delicately plucks me from H.H.'s purse, and I say, "See you tomorrow at Half Hour, H.H.?"

"Always," H.H. says.

"Always until May first," I say.

"That's a lot of preshows, Tiny. And we'll treasure them all." She pats me on the head, gives Stella's hand a comforting squeeze, wraps her light spring scarf around her neck with a flourish, and exits through the stage door like the goddess she is.

———◇———

MY BROTHERS, MOM, AND DAD ARE ALL WAITING DOWN-stairs in our nest.

"Please come in, Stella," my mom says. "I had Chris bring in a chair for you."

"You're too kind," Stella says. She deposits me with my family, then sits in the rickety wooden chair. A queen on her throne. A Tony winner in our home. (I know it's a stupid rhyme, but it made me feel better, so just go with it, okay?)

Laid out on the floor is a buffet of assorted dropped candies. Next to the buffet stand Walt and Matty, proudly admiring the fruits of their evening forage.

"Thought you might like some comfort food," Walt says.

"Someone snuck in Godiva tonight," Matty says. "Score, right?"

"Yeah," I say. "Thanks, guys."

I have zero interest in Godiva right now, proof that I am not myself today.

Wait a minute. It just hit me that my mother knew Stella was coming down here. She planned a chair delivery and everything. Which means she and Stella spoke during the show—and now I need to know what about.

"So, what's up, Stella?" I ask. "Aside from the fact that I ruined our show." I start to weep at this. Heaving, blubbering sobs, like someone pressed a giant CRY button and now it's stuck. My parents come over and put their arms around me. My brothers are looking around, unsure of what to do, how to comfort me. Matty offers up a salted caramel truffle and I swat it away.

"You did not ruin our show, Lulu," Stella says. "You brought it back to life."

"Then why are we closing?" I ask.

"Our ticket sales haven't been strong enough to stay open," Stella says. "We could sit here all day and try to figure out the reason."

"T. Mason," Timmy coughs out.

"T. Mason did have something to do with it, yes, Timothy," Stella says. "The point is: the powers that be have decided to close our show. But I've decided . . . I don't want to close."

"Well, I don't want to close either, but there's not much we can do about it," I say. By the way, even a month ago, I couldn't imagine being so blunt with Tony winner Stella James. I kind of can't believe the (sassy) words that just shot out of my mouth, but here we are. Up is down and left is right and I sass Tony winners with all my might. (The rhyming is helping me cope; go with it if you can.)

"I seem to remember a time when no mouse had ever performed on Broadway, and now, sitting here before me, is a mouse I had the privilege of performing with this very night. Here, at the Shubert Theatre, on Broadway." Stella descends her throne and sits down on the floor in front of me. "If anyone knows the merits of not giving up, it's you," Stella says. "I'm not ready to give up on this show, Lulu."

This woman. Wow. She could be anywhere, doing anything. She could be in Paris performing her solo concert. (Or casually people-watching and eating cheese and baguettes at a sidewalk café.) She could be on a television series or starring in a movie. She could be in just about any Broadway show she wants. But she wants to be here. In this show. With this company. With *me*.

"I'm glad you don't want to give up, but . . . when a show gets its closing notice, that's it, isn't it?"

"Maybe not," Benji says. "Stella and I—" He stops, looks at Stella, and says, "May I call you Stella?"

"Absolutely," Stella says.

"Stella and I were talking at intermission," Benji says. So it wasn't my mom who spoke with Stella, who set up this meeting. It was Benji. "And we think we have an idea."

"It's your idea, Benji, so please, continue," Stella says. She winks at my mom and dad, who are practically beaming with pride.

"Your first and second weeks onstage were our highest grossing since the week between Christmas and New Year's," Benji says. He turns toward Walt, Matty, and

Timmy and says, "That's typically the highest grossing week of the year for most shows."

Timmy shoots him an *I know, I read every show biz publication there is* glare, and Walt and Matty nod knowingly (though I'm certain they're confused by the word "grossing").

"It wasn't until T. Mason started writing all that mean stuff that audiences backed off," Benji says. "But at first, humans were psyched about the idea of seeing the first mouse to ever perform on Broadway. And if they could be psyched once, they can be psyched again."

"I guess that's true," I say. "But we can't exactly force them to buy tickets."

"We can't force them," Stella says. "But we can try to convince them."

"A *mouseroots* movement," Benji says.

"Like a play on 'grassroots'?" Timmy asks. "That's when everyday humans work together for a greater cause," Timmy says to Walt and Matty, who, again, nod knowingly.

"Exactly," Benji says. "We go back to basics. We, as a company, do the work. We get directly to ticket buyers and encourage them to see the show. We go to the TKTS booths, we stand out in front of our theatre—"

"I go on television and tell the world that they have the opportunity to see something truly special." Stella picks me up and holds me in the most comforting and loving way. "I tell the world that T. Mason lied. That the truth is, I couldn't be happier to be performing with Lulu the Broadway Mouse."

"You're not a novelty that's no longer novel, Lulu," Benji says. "You're *Show Boat*."

I know what my dear brother means, but I can tell by the look on Timmy's face that he's dying to explain the reference.

"*Show Boat* is considered the first Broadway musical," Timmy says. "The show that really made Broadway what it is. It opened the door for a Golden Age of Broadway, and everything we know and treasure today. Some might argue that *Oklahoma!* also had a hand in—"

The *that's enough, dear* look on my mom's face makes Timmy stop himself. "But that's a debate for another time."

"Beautifully said," Stella smiles. "You're the first, Lulu. Humans are always eager to witness a first."

"What if we do all this and the producers still decide that we're out of here in May?" I ask.

"At least we'll have tried," Stella says. "If there's one thing I've learned in my many years on this earth, it's that you never know until you try."

"How 'bout it, sis?" Benji asks. "You saved the day once. Ready to do it again?"

This is the moment in the movie when the camera would cut around to everyone in the room—my parents, my brothers, Stella. The camera would capture their reassuring, comforting looks and nods, and then finally land on me.

"Let's do this," I say.

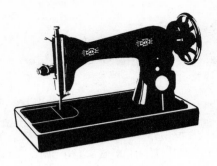

CHAPTER
EIGHTEEN

"O UR MISSION IS SIMPLE," BENJI SAYS, STRIDING around like a general giving orders to his soldiers. (Though a hint of Max Bialystock still lingers somewhere in the depths of this character.) "We target audience members who have yet to make their decision as to which show to see. Many of them will be out-of-towners, but there will be locals, too. This is a theatre town, after all."

It's Wednesday between shows, and our entire company is gathered in the lower lobby, thanks to an announcement Stella made after first calling Half Hour in Pete's place. "Ladies and gentlemen, this is your Half-Hour call."

At the sound of Stella's voice, Jodie yelled, "What's happening?" and was quickly shushed by H.H.

"In between shows, I invite you to join me in the lower lobby for a chat about the future. Dinner will be provided. Half Hour, please, Half Hour."

No one was naive enough to imagine that the producers suddenly had a change of heart, that's for sure. Throughout the show, I heard a lot of "She's so sweet to order dinner" and "It'll be nice to all be together," but no one expected a miracle. Still, they all made their way downstairs after our matinee, and now here we are, devouring Thai food and being instructed by Benji, our honorary producer, on how we'll save our show. The human members of our company know Benji well, so they're pretty accepting of his Mr. Producer routine.

"Of course, we need to be careful not to be too aggressive," Pete says.

"No one needs a lawsuit!" Jodie Howard advises.

"I will happily give everyone advice on how to toe the line between assertive and aggressive," H.H. says.

She shoots Lisa Logan a friendly (yet terrifying) stare and Lisa Logan replies, "We'll follow your lead, H.H.!" in a way that proves Lisa Logan now understands that H.H. is the one who decides on which side of the counter the tissue box sits.

"To build on what H.H. was saying," Benji says democratically, "if you approach someone at the TKTS booth, in front of the theatre, on the subway—"

"On the subway?" Olivia asks. "It's surprising you'd suggest the subway, Benji. That seems dangerous." Olivia is so small and so young, and yet she speaks with such confidence, it's almost charming. *Almost.*

"I only suggest the subway if you happen to be on your way to Times Square yourself, and you see that a rider is reading a map—that's a clue that the rider is a tourist—or you see them scrolling on a ticket app or the like. But most of the time, we'll focus on obvious ticket buyers, on solid ground."

"I think a good rule of thumb is that the kids can only approach someone if I'm with them," Milly says.

"Good idea," Benji says. "Okay, so. I thought we'd do a little experiment. It is currently . . ." Benji glances at the glowing Apple watch of a nearby chorus member, "five forty-two. Half Hour is at seven p.m. Anyone feel like taking a quick trip to the TKTS booth?"

"I'll do it," Harper says. "I'm not on tonight, right?" All of the principals Harper understudies shake their heads no. (Though, let's be honest, the Thai food will have the final say on that matter.)

"I'll go, too," Agnes says. "If we leave the TKTS booth by six fifty, we can be back by Half Hour."

"I'll join you!" an actor named Josh says. (P.S. Josh and Agnes are dating and they think they're keeping it a secret, but they're so not and I hope they get married.)

"Excellent," Benji says. "Remember. Keep it short and

sweet. Something like, 'We recently had a new performer join our cast. Perhaps you read about her debut in the *Times*? Her name is Lulu the Mouse. We're amazed by her, and we think you will be, too.'"

At this, I feel myself go from gray to blush. For a moment I wonder if my brother is doing all this for me, to lift my spirits and make me feel less "unappealing and unnecessary" (© T. Mason). But then Benji says, "Tomorrow, I'll check with the company manager to see how many tickets were sold via TKTS and we'll be able to gauge if we're on the right track or not," and I realize that although Benji might be doing this for me, he's also doing it for himself. For his dream. He wants to be a producer. The first mouse to ever hold the prestigious title. And saving a show from closing? That's quite the debut.

———◇———

ONCE THE HUMANS HAVE CLEANED UP ALL THE THAI food with a bit of help from the Hooligans (who might be the only souls in New York who actually like the bamboo that takes up so much space in Thai curries), my mother pulls me aside on my way up to my dressing room. "I need to speak with you for a moment, Lucy Louise." She walks me into the wardrobe room, where Bet stands steaming shirts for tomorrow's show.

"I didn't want to upset you in front of your friends," Mom says.

"What's wrong?" I ask. Please let it be something manageable, like Walt ate the fancy Italian cheese Bet bought to cheer me up. Please don't let it be something like—

"I know you want to participate in this *mouseroots* movement, as your brother so aptly named it," Mom says. "But I'm really not comfortable with you leaving the building."

"What? Why?" I ask.

"You know why," my mom says. "Humans don't—"

"Humans don't like mice?" I say. "Bet's a human; she likes me. Don't you, Bet?"

"Of course, I do," Bet says. "But that's not what your mother means."

"Humans liked me just fine when I was up there that first night with Jayne. The *Times* writer liked me. Everyone liked me until T. Mason told them they shouldn't."

"You being up on the stage is different from being out in the middle of Times Square, sweetheart," Mom says. "You're safe here, in the theatre. You're a part of the show. Out there . . . anything could happen."

I curl up next to her. Not to be manipulative, but because I can tell she needs a hug from her youngest.

"I know it's scary, Mom," I say. "But my castmates will take care of me."

"I know that," my mom says. "I trust them implicitly. It's the rest of humanity I'm worried about."

"Seeing me out there—it could sell a lot of tickets," I say.

I hear myself say *could*—it's telling that I used this word, instead of something certain like *will*. No matter how optimistic I try to be, there's still this little part of me that's worried our mouseroots movement will only make things worse. That my being so outgoing and up-front with my desire to perform on Broadway will cause humans to see me as entitled or spoiled or . . . too much. I realize that this whole time I've been giving humans a lot of credit. My only real experience with humans has taken place inside this building—this building that feels at all times as though it's humming with magic. I realize that it's very possible most humans are less like Bet and more like T. Mason.

"Or, it could hurt the cause," I say. "It could scare people off. Because they'd realize . . ."

"They'd realize what, my love?" Mom asks.

"They'd realize that we can talk."

Somehow, that hadn't occurred to me until now. My ability to converse with humans hasn't actually been acknowledged in the press. Sure, I sing onstage, but I don't wear a microphone, so I'm not loud enough for anyone in the audience to hear. What if it hasn't occurred to all those audience members, to all those non-theatre folk, that we mice actually speak to and converse with humans, and that if they choose to listen, they'll hear us? What if this fact is actually a far bigger story than me being allowed to be part of a Broadway show?

"If I do this, Mom, I change all of our lives, not just my own."

My mom raises up her eyes, like she does when she's contemplating the healthiest and least-damaging way to reply to her children.

"Are you glad you listened to Poppy, Bet?" Mom asks.

"I'd go back to 1944 and do it all over again," Bet says. "And I'm sure Poppy would, too."

Bet, you'll remember, was the first human to speak to a mouse, and that mouse was Poppy, who fulfilled her lifelong dream of sewing Broadway costumes because she was brave enough to trust a human.

"My ninety years have taught me this, Lulu," Bet says. "You almost always regret not taking a chance more than you regret taking it."

"What if . . . when I talk . . ." I say. "What if they don't like me?"

"What if they do like you?" Bet says. I feel her ninety years of wisdom wash over me like a warm bath.

Instead of agreeing with my worry, which would support her "Times Square is dangerous" argument, my mom says, "My little girl can charm the rind off an orange." (I generally eat an orange by biting its rind off in tiny, messy bits, but I appreciate the sentiment.)

Mom smiles and strokes my fur. "We all told you it wasn't possible, a mouse on Broadway. Because none of us—all these generations of mice living in these theatres—none of us had been brave enough to be the first to actually get up on that stage and perform. You proved us wrong. You changed our world for the better, Lucy Louise. And you'll do it again."

"The face of change," Bet says. "And quite a cute face, at that."

"I want you to keep being brave," Mom says. "I just want you to be careful and brave."

"'Carefully brave' sounds like something Sondheim would write," I say. (Mr. Sondheim, if you disagree, please feel free to pop over to the theatre and we'll discuss.) "How about this? Stella and I spoke about doing a trial run in Shubert Alley tomorrow—a PR event of sorts. It's an interview with the theatre critic for NY1." (NY1 is, to quote the play *Oh, Hello!* "the channel that comes on when you restart your cable box." But it also happens to feature some really fun and well-respected theatre segments, so it's a "big win" according to Stella's publicist.)

"Your father loves watching NY1 with Dan and Artie," Mom says. "He'll be thrilled."

"So, that's when I'll speak," I say. "I'll do it on camera, but the segment won't air until later that evening. That way, I'll be safely back in the theatre by the time New York City finds out we mice can speak to them. Just in case they freak out, or whatever."

"That sounds like a very reasonable plan," Mom says. "How'd my girl get so wise?"

"It runs in the family," I say.

"Half Hour, this is your Half-Hour call," Pete's voice alerts us via the intercom. "Half Hour, please, Half Hour."

"Gotta go," I say. "Love you, Mom."

"Love you, too, my Broadway Baby."

"Great song," I say.

"Sondheim." Mom nods.

"Remind me to tell you a story about *Follies*," Bet says. "Quite the story. Involves a broken zipper and some chewing gum."

"Can't wait," I say. (Side note: How have I not heard this story before?!) "By the way, Bet, love you, too."

"And you, my dear."

Bet keeps steaming shirts, and my mom gets to work

sewing a missing button onto a shirt that's waiting to be steamed.

I scurry out of the wardrobe room, leaving behind its warmth and freshness, and head up the stairs that lead to the main level of the theatre. Rosa is at the stage door. "I hear you're going to save the show," she says.

"I'm sure gonna try."

"I can't think of a time it's happened before," Rosa says. "But there's a first time for everything."

I make my way up the stairs to Jodie and H.H.'s dressing room, but I don't go in right away. I just sit there in the doorway, watching them. They're seated side by side, their heads pin-curled and wig-capped—they look like gorgeous bald eagles. Jodie is jabbering away about how the publicity from our mouseroots movement could really help when it comes to her negotiations for *Apartment* and how she's sure she could make both jobs work; and H.H. is sitting there nodding, lining her eyes, calm and content—for the moment, at least—in her role as sounding board for her whirling dervish of a best friend. Yesterday at this time, I thought moments like these were numbered. And they still are, I suppose; even if we save our show, it will close eventually, as all shows do. But, like Stella, I'm not ready to give up on this show just yet. Backstage, onstage—I'm not ready to let it go.

(Naturally, though, I am ready to *sing* "Let It Go.")

"Tiny," H.H. says. "How long are you going to linger in that doorway? My lashes aren't going to glueify themselves."

I'll do just about anything for more moments like these.

Even if "just about anything" means talking on television and revealing a secret that could change everything.

My mom said I should. Bet, the human who's known me longer than any other human, told me I should.

So I will.

I'm a talking mouse, and I have a lot to say.

NY1, here I come.

CHAPTER
NINETEEN

W E FIND THAT THE MOMENT WE TURN on the camera, people surround us." Bernard Bradshaw, the NY1 anchor who will be interviewing us, says these words in a way that makes me think he's both thrilled with and exhausted by his job.

People surround us. It's not exactly what a mouse normally wants to hear, but, then again, I'm not a normal mouse. I hope people surround us, and I hope it leads to ticket sales. Lots and lots of ticket sales.

"Well," Stella says calmly, giving my head a comforting pat, "attention is the goal."

We're in Shubert Alley, just outside the stage door, and Stella has me cupped in her palms. Ricardo is with us to represent stage management and the production, and tucked into Ricardo's jacket is Benji. We agreed I'll be the only mouse to speak, but he thought it was important he be here to observe and intervene, in case Stella and I don't hit all of our talking points. (But it's me and Stella, so . . . we'll hit all of our talking points and more.)

I've only ever been out here for a few seconds before running back inside, because until today I wasn't technically allowed outside the building. And I'll tell you: my Shubert has itself quite the alley—it's so much more fabulous than what I can see from out my third-floor window. The entire length of Shubert Alley is lined with posters of current Broadway shows. Between our stage door and the Booth Theatre's stage door is a cute little book and theatre merchandise store. But the alley accessory that's my absolute favorite is a bronze sign, decorated with the comedy and drama masks, that reads:

"SHUBERT ALLEY"
DEDICATED TO ALL THOSE
WHO GLORIFY THE THEATRE
AND USE THIS SHORT THOROUGHFARE

Yes, of course reading this makes me tear up; I'm a theatre-loving mouse, not a monster. But I will recover before I make my television debut. Which is—judging by the way Bernard Bradshaw is checking his teeth and straightening his bowtie—moments away from happening. I take this opportunity to straighten out my chartreuse ribbon scarf and smooth my fur. I wasn't going to wear my scarf, for fear it might look a bit gimmicky, but Stella said it makes me look "relatable yet chic." After a review like that from Tony winner Stella James, did I really have a choice in the matter?

Bernard Bradshaw looks down at me, smiles with his pristine teeth, and says, "She's charming." He says it in a way, though, that makes me think he's both excited for and weirded out by this exclusive interview. He's face-to-face with a mouse. I don't need to tell you what normally happens when humans come face-to-face with a mouse. This isn't a scary movie.

"Before we begin," Stella says, "I want to be clear on a few things."

"Of course," Bernard Bradshaw says. "Of course."

"Lulu isn't here for decoration," Stella says. "Just as she's not there for decoration onstage."

"Of course," the anchor says. "She dances! I saw her in action when I came to the show last week. A dancing mouse. How that's not more of a draw I don't know."

I look up at Stella, and she nods. To quote Frank Wildhorn's *Jekyll & Hyde*, "This is the moment." My first time talking to a human outside of the theatre. Rosa just emerged from the stage door and is standing in the door-way watching us, so if this anchor guy freaks out, I can be into the safety of Rosa's arms and our stage door threshold faster than you can say "*Wicked* was a wise investment."

I take a deep breath and say, "I seemed to be quite the draw until T. Mason got involved."

NY1 anchor Bernard Bradshaw looks like he swallowed a bug.

"Are you all right, Bernard?" Stella asks.

"She talks," Bernard says. He looks at me, cocks his head like a dog reacting to an offer for a walk, and says, "You talk?"

"Yep," I say. "And I can sing, too." I sing this sentence to the melody of "I Can Cook, Too" from *On the Town.*

A few passersby have slowed their speed and are lingering near us, trying to figure out what's happening. Bernard Bradshaw puts his arm on Stella's shoulder and turns her so we're huddled toward the Shubert, and I'm hidden from view.

"Mice can talk?" Bernard asks.

"Yes," I say.

"And sing?" he asks.

"Well, some can," I say. "I sing better than most, just like Stella sings better than most humans." Stella cracks a close-up-worthy sly smile at my confident declaration.

Bernard Bradshaw's face shifts—like the bug he just swallowed has turned into the most delicious thing he's ever tasted.

"So, what you're telling me is, mice can talk, they can sing, you're a mouse who's singing on Broadway, and I'm the journalist who gets to break this story to the world?"

"That's exactly right," Stella says. "You have always been a favorite of mine, Bernard."

The look on this guy's face is what my face would look like if I heard "And the Tony goes to Lulu the Mouse." Bernard Bradshaw has decided that me talking means he's struck gold. The musical theatre version of him would be breaking into bell kicks right about now.

"Let's get to it then, if you're ready, Stella?"

Bernard Bradshaw waves to his cameraman, who's been waiting across the alley. The cameraman lifts his camera up onto his shoulder in a way that makes me think he is most certainly exhausted by his job, and he lumbers toward us.

"Absolutely," Stella says. "Ready, Lulu?"

"Yep," I say. I see Bet make her way through the stage door. She's wearing one of her signature old Italian lady housecoats. This one is dark gray, with some pink flowers. The colors beautifully camouflage my mother inside Bet's pocket. But I see her, because I always see my mother.

She pops her head all the way out of the pocket and smiles at me—the kind of smile I imagine a mom gives her kid as they head off to their first day of school. She's proud of me and excited for me, but she's also nervous. I look back at her, nod an *it's going to be okay, Mom* nod, then look back at Bernard Bradshaw and say, "Let's get this show on the road."

This makes Bernard laugh. "Well, all right, then, here we go."

The cameraman is next to us now, and Bernard whispers something into his ear, to which the cameraman replies, "Yeah, right, and my kid's guinea pig plays the accordion," so . . . Mr. Cameraman is in for a big surprise when I open my mouth.

He adjusts the camera on his shoulder and silently counts, "Three, two, one," then points his finger at Bernard Bradshaw.

"I'm here in Shubert Alley, with two-time Tony Award winner Stella James," Bernard says. "A pleasure, as always, Stella."

"The pleasure is all mine," Stella says.

"We're very sorry to hear your show is closing," Bernard says. "I, for one, loved it. Viewers will recall my glowing review from our segment that aired just after opening night."

He looks at Stella like he's expecting a thank you, but instead Stella says, "This show is a beautiful one. It should continue to be seen and experienced. And one of the biggest reasons to buy a ticket is this young lady right here."

Stella lifts her hands up in front of her chest. "This is Lulu. She joined our show in late January, and her performance is really something everyone should witness."

"A mouse on Broadway," Bernard says. "Certainly a new experience, even for the most seasoned theatre-goer."

The anchor points his microphone toward me, but, huh, that's weird. All I can do is smile and nod.

"Perhaps Lulu has something to say about her debut?" Bernard asks.

This makes the cameraman grunt out a laugh; Bernard Bradshaw sends him a glare so sharp it could cut a watermelon clean in half.

Bernard shoves the microphone toward me again, and he cocks his head and widens his eyes, in a manner that's encouraging but just a smidge too intense.

Why can't I speak? I've been looking forward to my television debut for forever. But the camera's lights, plus the fact that a crowd has started to gather, appear to have zapped my ability to speak. Sure, I've been a bit nervous to talk in front of regular non-theatrical humans, but I thought I was ready. Stage fright and I have never really been a thing. But there's something about this camera being four feet from my face that has me queasy and nervous—like I'm in a museum devoted solely to cat art—and I really need to snap out of it.

Stella seems to sense my sudden unease and continues talking, buying me a little time to get my act together.

"Lulu and dear Jayne Griffin, our new young leading lady, are truly reasons to see our show—even if you've seen it before," Stella says. "We here at the Shubert believe in this production, so much so that we're hoping to sell enough tickets over the next few weeks to convince our producers to keep us open."

Behind the cameraman is Ricardo; Benji has wiggled his way into Ricardo's sleeve, so only his head is popping out the arm hole. And that head is nodding approvingly at Stella—thrilled that she's hitting all of his talking points.

"Quite a lofty goal," Bernard Bradshaw says. "I can't say I've ever heard of a cast saving its show before."

"This isn't just any show," Stella says. "For many reasons. But reason number one is sitting right here in my hands. I've shared the stage with many unique performers, but never one like this young lady. The first mouse ever to perform on Broadway. I'm thrilled to be a part of this history-making moment."

"Absolutely," the anchor says. "And, Lulu? Lulu the Broadway Mouse, as you've been named by so many of our newspapers. Do you think saving your show is possible?"

This question makes Chuckles the Cameraman snort with laughter.

Benji looks at me, exclamation marks dancing around his head, and mouths the word, "Speak!"

Stella gives my head a comforting pat. I take a deep breath and I say something I've said to you before, dear reader, so pardon me for reusing it.

"Plenty of things never happened until they did."

At this, Bernard Bradshaw smiles, and says, "That's very true, Lulu."

The cameraman manages not to drop his camera, which truly is a miracle, because his jaw looks like it's about to hit the floor and make him topple forward.

Bernard Bradshaw sends an *I told you so* look to the cameraman, then redirects all of his focus toward me.

"Viewers, you heard it here first on *It's Broadway with Bernard Bradshaw*. You heard this mouse, this dancing, singing mouse, you heard her speak. Live. Exclusively here, on NY1."

Wow. Bernard Bradshaw is loving this.

"If you don't mind, Bernard, Lulu has a few things she'd like to say to your viewers," Stella says.

"The first mouse ever to speak to humans on television would like to say something and so she shall," Bernard says. "As the host of *It's Broadway with Bernard Bradshaw*, I give you all the time you need to say what you need to say, Lulu. The Broadway Mouse."

Stella nods a *calm down, Bernard* nod, and I look over at the cameraman, to make sure he's not going to collapse and miss this shot. He's upright, for now, so I look at Bernard and say, "I'm not going to stand here and tell you I'm just like every other performer. Because I'm not. I'm different. And that's *why* you should come to our show. Be here to witness something that's never happened before."

"Support something that's different from what we're used to," Bernard says.

"Exactly," I say. I look directly into the camera's lens—which is appropriate for interviews, but not for on-camera acting—and, with all the hope, heart, and chutzpah I can muster, I say, "Hello, New York. It's nice to meet you. I know the idea of a talking mouse might be scary to you, but there's no need to be afraid. Because we actually have a lot in common. And one of those things is that, like me, you all have dreams, too. I know you do. If you had finally achieved your dream, against all odds, after a lifetime of being told it wouldn't happen, wouldn't you do whatever you could to save that dream? And wouldn't you help others save theirs? Viewers of NY1: this is your chance to help me save my dream. And the dreams of all the people—"

I look at Benji in Ricardo's sleeve, revise my noun and say, "—the dreams of all the *souls* in this building." I motion to the Shubert in the hope that Chuckles-No-More the Cameraman will pan up to capture just how gorgeous my home is, and then I say, "Don't regret not taking the chance."

"Beautifully put, Lulu," Stella says. "Bernard, I hope you and all your viewers understand now why I'm fighting so hard to save this show."

"Absolutely, of course, of course," he says. "'Plenty of things never happened until they did' is going to be my mantra from now on!" He turns to the camera and says, "Head on over to the Shubert Theatre on Forty-Fourth Street between Broadway and Eighth Avenue to see a stellar show, a cast that won't quit, and Lulu the Broadway Mouse, who is living proof that anything can happen. This is *It's Broadway with Bernard Bradshaw*, NY1."

The light on the camera shuts off and the cameraman walks slowly over to us.

"She's not real, right?" he says to Stella.

"Why don't you ask her?" Stella says.

The cameraman does something I thought only happened in movies. He gulps.

"You're not real, right?" he asks.

I shake my head and say, "Wrong."

The cameraman does something else I thought only happened in movies. He faints.

"Oh, goodness, Gerald," Bernard Bradshaw says. "Don't be so dramatic."

A crowd has gathered now, and people are saying things like "What's happening?" and "Is that man all right?" and "That guy from the news is quite handsome." A little boy looks up at his mom and says, "Can we see the show with the talking mouse?" to which she replies, "Anything to get you to stop playing video games for five minutes," and they veer away from us toward the box office!

Ricardo and Benji hurry over, both with huge smiles on their faces.

"Why don't you take them both inside, Ricardo," Stella says. "People are starting to get just a bit too close."

She's right—the crowd is growing by the minute, and now I'm hearing things like "I can't believe it and I won't believe it" and "Who does that little mouse think she is?" But these negative comments—these T. Mason–adjacent comments—are the minority. Most people seem excited by the idea of me. I'm hearing a lot of "She's adorable" and "I thought I'd seen everything!" and "It's like *The Lion King,* but real!" Hopefully, the feedback from tonight's episode of *It's Broadway with Bernard Bradshaw* will be mostly positive as well.

"I should probably make sure Gerald the Cameraman is all right," Stella says. She hands me to Ricardo and saunters toward Bernard Bradshaw, who seems to have revived Gerald.

I snuggle into Ricardo's left sleeve. Out of his right

sleeve Benji says, "Well, it was a rocky start, sis, but you finished strong." (Is this sports terminology? It feels like sports terminology.)

Ricardo, who's rather tall, turns his attention toward Forty-Fourth Street and says, "Would you look at that?" He lifts us up to his height, so we can see what he's seeing.

A line has formed at our box office and around the side of the building.

A *long* line.

"It's working," Benji says.

It's working.

———◇———

It's Friday evening after the show, and I'm sipping some celebratory Martinelli's sparkling apple cider out of a bottle cap because, guess what?

"Harper, Agnes, and Josh's very short Wednesday TKTS trip amounted to thirty tickets sold," Benji says.

"Thursday we were up twenty percent from the week before, with nine hundred eighty-five bodies in seats, at an average ticket price of $119, and tonight's audience count was one thousand two hundred twenty-nine. As you know, we have one thousand four hundred forty-seven seats at the Shubert, which means we were eighty-five percent full. Not bad for a Friday in early spring."

"That's a lot of numbers," Walt says. He hands the granola bar he's a bite away from finishing over to Matty.

Matty looks at the measly portion and grumbles, "Yeah. Simplify, Benj. Simplify."

"All those numbers mean we're on our way," I say.

"You certainly are," my dad says. "Very impressive, you two."

"Our children can do anything!" my mom says. She's zipping around our nest distributing new sticky-note-sized blankets to all of us—made out of scraps of velvet ribbon she sewed together during yesterday's and today's shows. Her clandestine trip into Shubert Alley really stoked her spirit. "Bless those non-theatre people and their open minds!"

"Bless the members of this company who have been pounding the pavement over at the TKTS booth," I say. "I'll go with them tomorrow."

"And I'll go with you," my dad says.

"I'll be fine with H.H.," I say.

"It's not up for discussion, Lulu," Dad says.

"Mom told me I could go."

"And your father's not telling you you can't," Mom says. "Just that he's going with you. The segment on NY1 means that people now know you can talk. We need to be careful, that's all. Besides, Jayne and Olivia don't traipse around New York City alone, either."

"I already spoke with Pete," Dad says. "I'm going to ride along in his fanny pack."

Yes, Pete rocks a fanny pack from time to time. Around his waist. Like he's a dad in an eighties movie.

Let's continue.

"You won't even know I'm there, unless something happens and you need me," Dad says.

He's not being unreasonable, I suppose. I am really young and small. It is a really big city. And, thanks to Bernard Bradshaw's segment last night on NY1, humans are bound to be more fascinated by me than they were before. I do maintain that H.H. could sufficiently protect me, but I'm my parents' only girl—and favorite offspring—plus, the success of this show now rides on my shoulders. If people showed up to the theatre expecting to see Lulu the Mouse only to hear that Teddy the (Stuffed) Bear would be taking my place, I imagine they'd expect a refund. They'd tweet angrily, word of mouth would be terrible . . . yes, I know I'm flattering myself, but just go with it, okay? (Thanks.)

The moral of the story is: for the sake of our show, it's best if my dad joins us at the TKTS booth tomorrow. So glad I made this decision.

"Okay," I say. "Sounds good, Dad."

"While you're all there, I'm going to be in the box office," Benji says.

"You don't want to join us at the TKTS booth?" my dad asks.

"I don't need to be in the spotlight," Benji says. "That's Lulu's role."

If I ever complain about my brother again, please remind me of this very moment.

"Where should we be?" Walt asks. "What are our roles?"

"Yeah," Matty says. "We want to help, too." He burps. "We'll come to Times Square."

Let's pause right here. Just for a second. My mind just jumped to a musical, which it's prone to do. I'm reminded of the second act of *Kiss Me, Kate,* when the two gangster characters—the comedic relief of the show—have a big number out in front of the curtain, just the two of them. It's called "Brush Up Your Shakespeare," and once your parent or guardian gives you permission, you really should listen to the cast recording—I recommend the one featuring the exquisite Marin Mazzie—because *Kiss Me, Kate* is a stellar example of Cole Porter's lyric-writing abilities.

Anyway . . . somehow it never occurred to me before, but if my brothers were to play any roles on Broadway, they'd play these scene-stealing gangsters. Just two wise-cracking, one-upping, nothing's-off-limits-for-comedy characters. Let's imagine, for a moment, what would happen if they joined me and my humans in Times Square. The front-page articles would read something like this . . .

Brothers of Lulu the Broadway Mouse Wreak Havoc at the Times Square TKTS Booth

Humans of the Shubert Theatre were joined by Lulu the Broadway Mouse on Saturday to promote their show and encourage ticket sales. But Lulu's brothers—Walter Brooks and Matthew—took things a bit too far. Escorted by two cast members, Walt and Matty, as they're known to the Shubert employees, reportedly heckled any ticket buyers who said they'd prefer to see a different show. "*Hamilton?* Not gonna happen, my friend." "*Aladdin?* Just watch the movie!" One of them reportedly yelled, "There's only one show in town, New York!" then jumped into the arms of a young ticket buyer, who was eating a soft pretzel. The young ticket buyer promptly flung the mouse onto another ticket buyer, which began a chaotic scene that can only be described as *Humans of New York Play Hot Potato with Heckling Mouse*. Ticket buyers fled the TKTS booth and surrounding area, leading to a loss in ticket sales, not only for the Shubert's show, but for all shows in general.

You get the picture, right? Walt and Matty joining us in Times Square cannot happen. The fact that we mice can talk to humans was revealed only twenty-four hours ago. It's probably best if they only hear from me, at least for the time being. Adjusting to new life rules takes time, especially for humans.

I look at my mom, widen my eyes, and slowly shake my head NO. My brothers don't see me because they're busy picking crumbs off of each other's fur and eating them. I'm. Not. Kidding.

"You two can help me make dinner," Mom says. "And making dinner doesn't mean collecting candy. If your sister can perform on Broadway and your brother can sell tickets in the box office, you two can certainly learn how to make a healthy dinner. You can support this mouseroots movement by making sure your siblings have full bellies."

A random assignment, sure, but my mother's no fool. Walt and Matty shouldn't be allowed anywhere near our ticket-selling venture. They always take things a smidge too far. Also, I think my parents are tired of making dinner.

"I call sous chef!" Matty says.

"Aw, man," Walt says. "I don't want to work for you."

I don't have the heart to tell my brothers that *sous* means "under" in French and that a sous chef actually works for a chef. They'll figure it out. Eventually.

Besides, I'm distracted by Timmy over in the corner of our living room. He's been reading contentedly on Pete's old iPad—he "turns" pages by what can only be described as a tap dance–moonwalk combo—but upon moonwalking to the next article, his expression has changed from enjoyment to disappointment, like he's a living theatre mask.

"What's up?" I ask Timmy. "Did someone use an apostrophe to pluralize a word? Or confuse *their, there,* and *they're?*"

"No, it's . . ." He looks at our parents like he's asking for their help.

"What is it, sweetheart?" my mom asks. She scurries over to him, and although our mom isn't the speed reader Timmy is, she quickly clocks the words on the page that are causing Timmy so much distress.

"Not again," my mom says. She looks like she wants to rip something. Tear something. And not sew it back together. I know what's on the iPad. *Who's* on the iPad.

"T. Mason," I say.

THEATRE THOUGHTS with T. Mason

Talk about a publicity stunt. From company members practically begging at the TKTS booths to Stella James appearing with her show's token TALKING mouse on television's least-watched station . . . it's pathetic. Desperate. Inappropriate. In my day, when a show was given its closing notice, a company accepted the news and moved on. What if each auditioning actor was told they didn't get the job, only to show up at rehearsal? In my day, when a performer was told their dream was dead, they took their lumps and moved on. And despite what you've heard, this is not the first scheme of this company to keep their show open. I have it on good authority that Lulu the Mouse's seemingly spontaneous debut was planned. The show's ticket sales had been slow since autumn, and the powers that be thought, "What better way to drum up some attention? Put a mouse onstage. But make it look like an accident." Sources tell me that this mouse was rehearsed, that Amanda Rose Green was paid extra to miss the show that evening, and that Jayne Griffin was told she had to work with the mouse, or she'd never go on again. What a sham. Let's go back to the way things were, New York, don't you think? Back to when artists took no for an answer and moved on. Back to when mice stayed silent, in the basement and in the sewers, where they belong. Hear me now, New York. No to this scheme. No to this "dream." No to Lulu the Mouse.

CHAPTER
TWENTY

H ELLO, THERE. DO YOU KNOW WHAT SHOW
you're seeing today?"

"Are you . . . ? You're Stella James!" a tourist croons to Stella. (I'm guessing he's a tourist because
he has the same accent as the characters in *Waitress*.)
"Everyone! *The* Stella James is here!"

From my secure location inside H.H.'s purse, I hear
the crowd begin to hum. One person goes, "Who?" but
other than that, people seem to know her. H.H. whispers
to me, "People are starting to film us."

At the Times Square TKTS booth in between shows
this Saturday are me, Stella, H.H., Milly, Jayne, Olivia,

Pete, and Susie. (My dad is safely tucked away in Pete's fanny pack, and I truly do believe he'll stay there unless someone tries to kidnap me or something.)

We hadn't initially planned on Stella joining because she usually likes to rest after a matinee, but when she arrived at the theatre at a quarter to twelve on Saturday, she announced she'd be coming along. She was calm, per usual, but I could tell by the straightness of her spine and the height of her heels that she wasn't about to let T. Mason win this round. A Tony-winning legend at the TKTS booth on a Saturday between shows? *Plenty of things never happened until they did,* indeed.

Speaking of things that never happened until they did: did I mention *I'm* in *Times Square*? I haven't quite seen it yet, but I'm here! Fairly certain I'll burst into "NYC" from *Annie* or "Not for the Life of Me" from *Thoroughly Modern Millie* when I finally emerge from H.H.'s purse and get a glimpse of this great big glorious apple.

Though it doesn't smell like an apple. It smells like Starbucks and car exhaust and hot dogs and . . . wait . . . give me a second. . . . Oooh yeah, no, that's not a smell you want me to describe.

"What's your name?" Stella asks the tourist.

"Brian," he says. "I'm from South Carolina."

(Told ya.)

"Well, Brian from South Carolina," Stella says, "am I correct in assuming you're looking to see a show this evening?"

"Yes, ma'am," I hear a voice similar to Brian's say. "We saw your show the last time we visited New York, Ms. James."

"Why are you here?" a voice calls out. The body behind this voice is . . . hmm . . . I'm going to go with that it's from Boston. He sounds like the mailman from that *Cheers* show Bet likes to watch while she sorts laundry.

"My castmates and I are here to encourage you to see our show," Stella says.

"It's the best show on Broadway," Olivia says. It's an improvised moment from outgoing Olivia, but I can't argue with her.

"When she's right, she's right," Stella says. The crowd laughs approvingly, Olivia (I assume) glows with pride, and Stella continues. "You're all here because you want to experience live theatre. And bravo to you for that. Thank you for supporting the arts. If you've yet to decide what to see, we encourage you to see our show. Because ours has something to offer that others don't."

That's my cue. Times Square debut in three, two—

"We have Lulu the Mouse," H.H. says proudly. And then, faster than you can say "Please YouTube Liza Minnelli singing 'New York, New York,'" I'm out of H.H.'s purse and face-to-face with a sight I never thought I'd see.

Times Square.

Oh. Wow.

The crowd gasps. But their awe only feeds H.H.'s performance. She pauses, then coolly and confidently says,

"Lulu the *Broadway* Mouse—the first mouse to ever perform on Broadway."

Lulu the Broadway Mouse. The first of her siblings to see Times Square.

Let's talk about this for a moment.

Of course I've seen pictures of it. Videos—old and new. But actually being here, experiencing it for the first time? *Feeling* it for the first time? I feel like a bee in a beehive. There are just so many bodies here. All different colors and ages and sizes. Speaking of size, these billboards are *huge*. Some are static posters, some are moving screens, flashing advertisements for television shows and perfume and—oh, look, a giant M&M! And—oohh, yeah, those humans dressed up in dirty Elmo and Batman costumes are just as scary as Jayne said they were. I could do without them, to be honest.

My goodness it's bright out here. A different kind of bright than I'm used to. Our Shubert lights are cozy; these lights are alarming. Everything here feels so striking and distracting. So buzzy and harsh. But it's all so beautiful, in its own way. I see what all the fuss is about.

Speaking of fuss . . . the crowd at the TKTS booth is massive and growing rapidly, and all eyes are on us. I'm not exaggerating when I tell you everyone is holding up their phones. I'm usually not super into technology, but in this moment, I am so thankful for these phone-camera hybrids. I'm thankful for social media, all the apps I don't understand how to use. Because the videos these people are filming will go out to all the people they know. People in California who are coming into New York next week will know that there is a mouse performing onstage at the Shubert. Kids in Philadelphia who dream of Broadway will see this video and beg their parents to drive them to New York to see the Broadway show with the kids and the mouse. Stella James fans will respect her commitment to her job, her company, her friends. They will be inspired.

I hope.

It's possible all of this will backfire. That bullies like T. Mason will win out. But, for now, we're trying. For now, we're pushing through all the chatter and all the lies and all the messiness that comes when art and money collide, and we're here. Together. In Times Square. Making history as the first company to welcome a mouse to their stage. Making history as the first company who won't leave their stage without a (peaceful) fight.

"So we hope you all will join us at the Shubert. Today, tonight, tomorrow. Next week . . . we hope to see you. Brian, I hope you and your—well, I hope you're a couple because you make a very handsome one."

"Engaged," guy-who-sounds-like-Brian says.

"Splendid," Stella says. "I hope you lovebirds will consider coming to our show again. Our new cast member is worth a return ticket."

"We're buying tickets for tonight!" South Carolina Brian yells.

"I'm so glad to hear it," Stella says. "And thank you,

all, for listening. I only have one more thing to say, and I want it on the record."

I am *floored* by the fact that this too-big-to-count gaggle of humans has remained gathered around us for this long, and that they're all listening attentively to this tiny Tony winner. I knew she was special, but this is pure magic. (Side note: that no one has tried to poison me or trap me with cheese or peanut butter is also magic, yes?)

"For those of you who read T. Mason's latest column, or have heard of it, please know that nothing written there is true," Stella says. "T. Mason, I invite you to visit me, Lulu, and the rest of our company at the Shubert, to really know us, so you can write facts instead of fiction."

A tall, old lady, standing next to her tall, old husband, says, "That's the mouse from the television. That's the mouse from the television, Stu."

"That mouse was a puppet. It talked. This mouse is real. Look at it," Stu says.

"The mouse on TV was real," a little girl says

confidently. "You're her, aren't you? You really can talk, right, Lulu?"

I look at the little girl and then up at H.H. She says, "Now's your inning, Tiny. Stand the world on its ear." What she just said is almost a direct quote from *Gypsy*, though Mr. Sondheim didn't write in "Tiny"—that's all H.H. My H.H.

Stella nods calmly and certainly.

My dad pops his head out of Pete's fanny pack and with my supersonic mouse ears I hear him say, "There's nothing to be afraid of. I'm right here."

I nod back at him, look at the little girl, and say, "I really can talk."

The crowd gasps in unison, like a giant taking a breath. Immediately, we lose a dozen or so people. A talking mouse and they're out of here like a home run into left field. (Sports!) But most people stay. They might be scared, they might be confused or grossed out or intrigued or captivated or angry, but whatever it is they're feeling, those feelings have led to the decision to stay. To listen to me, Lulu the (Talking) Broadway Mouse.

"I knew it," the little girl says. "I just knew it."

There's something in this little girl's eyes that gives me the one drop of courage I was missing. But I've got it now, and my dad's right there, so I'm ready to say what I want and need to say. There's nothing like knowing that a stranger has your back.

I summon all the breath power I can, and project into the crowd. "Earlier this year I learned that humans aren't mean for no reason. I know something's going on with you, T. Mason, to make you write the things you have. And while your words have done a lot of damage to us . . . to me . . . I'm here to say, I'm sorry you're hurt. Or angry. Or frustrated. I'm here if you want to talk it all out. Please don't be afraid of me, because I'm not afraid of you."

A beat that feels as long as the second act of a bad play, then . . .

Cheers. Applause. Whistles. (Which is fine, because we're outside.)

They are cheering for hope. They are whistling for chutzpah. They are applauding the idea of never giving up. Of trying, of being better, of being kind. Of being different.

Whatever happens to our production, what we're doing *matters*. It's bigger than me and my dream. When I dreamed of my Broadway debut, I never dreamed of a mouseroots movement to go with it.

The applause begins to lighten, as people return to their phones, eager to post about what just happened on a spring Saturday in Times Square. Post away, everybody! Spread this video around like it's the flu in February!

"I think that went very well," Stella says to the group. "Let's get back to the theatre. We have a show to do."

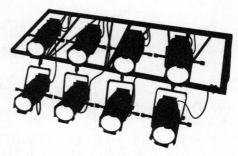

CHAPTER
TWENTY-ONE

THE CURTAIN CAME DOWN ON OUR WEDNESDAY matinee about ten minutes ago, so that means it's T. Mason time. Yep. T. Mason is coming to our theatre. To talk. *Plenty of things never happened until they did,* squared.

"But how does Stella know it's really T. Mason?" Olivia asks. "It could be someone posing as T. Mason. It could be a person who wants to hurt us or steal from us or hold us hostage for ransom."

A comment like this is exactly the evidence Milly needs to prove to Olivia's parents that she shouldn't be listening to true crime podcasts while she does her homework backstage.

"Stella's publicist vetted the situation," I say. I'm up on Jayne's dressing room counter, staring into the mirror, trying to get my chartreuse ribbon scarf to drape evenly.

"It feels like we're in some sort of spy novel," Jayne says. She pulls a baseball hat over her wig-capped head so she won't have to re-pin-curl her hair before this evening's show. "It's all so exciting."

"Do you think it's a guy or a girl?" Olivia asks.

"A man or a woman, you mean?" Milly says. "T. Mason has been writing since I was a baby."

"The gender of this person doesn't matter," I say. "Mean is mean is mean."

"What does matter is that he or she is taking this first brave step," Jayne says. "The bully and the bullied, together in the Shubert's star dressing room. It could really work out. Look at how things ended up with Amanda."

"You're right," I say. "Here's hoping I end up with another unexpected friend."

"I don't understand why we can't join," Olivia says.

"Because we weren't invited," Milly says. "And because we're going to 5 Napkin Burger for dinner. Jackets on, girls. I made a reservation."

Jayne and I follow behind Olivia and Milly, down the stairs to the stage level of the theatre. We land right between the stage door and the entrance to Stella's dressing room. Rosa is at her post watching the beginning of the five o'clock news.

"This is where we leave you," Jayne says. "It's going to be all right."

"Better than all right," Milly says. "This meeting is absolutely a step in the right direction."

"If I have any french fries left over, I'll bring them back for you," Olivia says. It's her way of saying she's there for me. And guess what? I'll take it.

I make my way into Stella's dressing room, where I find my mom, Bet, and Chris. My mom insisted on being with me for this meeting, which I get. And Stella suggested Bet be here, too, since she's "the wisest person in the building."

"Does this chartreuse ribbon scarf make me look adorable or desperate?" I ask.

"Adorable," my mom says.

"And very sophisticated," Bet says.

Per Bet's suggestion, my mom brought along her very own anger management prop: a patchwork of old scraps she's sewn together and will rip apart in quiet frustration if things don't go well with T. Mason. The mouse version of screaming into or punching a pillow, I guess.

The dressing room door opens and we all turn in fraught anticipation, but it's only Stella, returning from signing autographs in the alley. Like Rosa would ever let T. Mason barge right into Stella's dressing room. I mean, really.

"Ladies," Stella says. "And Chris."

"Don't worry," Chris says. "I'm leaving. And I'm taking this laundry with me." Stella James's ditty bag in hand, Chris turns to me and says, "No matter what this witch or mister witch says, never forget that you are a blessed light for which we are all grateful."

Stella's assistant, Trish, pops her head into Stella's dressing room.

"T. Mason is here," she says.

"Well, Chris, as usual, you timed things perfectly," Bet says.

"Ain't my first rodeo," Chris says. "Shine your light, Lulu." And he's off.

Rosa was the first to see T. Mason. Then Trish. Now Chris. Next up? Two mice and two ladies who have spent more time in Broadway theatres than they have anywhere else in the world. It feels right that we should be the first thespians to uncover T. Mason's true identity.

Faster than you can say "Not every movie should be turned into a Broadway musical," the dressing room door opens and behind Trish stands T. Mason.

I don't know what I expected, really.

Ink-stained hands? A furrowed brow? The witch from *Into the Woods*?

T. Mason is the smallest human in the room. She's wearing a light spring coat and an actual bonnet—like she's a *Downton Abbey* maid on her day off or something. It's chic, somehow, in a costume kind of way. Age-wise, I'd guess she's just a smidge older than H.H. (Don't tell H.H.)

For a few counts of eight, we all just look at each other. I really don't like to judge people by their appearance, but I must say, it's not a shock that T. Mason has had her column for thirty years or so and no one has ever figured out who she is. Because T. Mason looks about as intimidating as a bar of soap.

"We're so glad you're here," Stella says. "Won't you sit down?" She motions to her dressing room chair.

"Thank you," T. Mason says. "Please, call me Tabitha."

"Tabitha," Stella says. "We're so grateful you agreed to meet with us."

"So grateful," I say.

"So it's real, then," Tabitha says. "You can talk."

"Thanks for listening," I say.

Tabitha lowers her chin in an elegant, angled way, then nods delicately. "I almost turned around and went home when I saw the stage door." Admitting she's scared— this is good, Team. This is a promising sign.

"It must be a tough building to walk by," Bet says. "Disappointments like yours often linger for a lifetime."

Tabitha looks at Bet as though she hadn't truly noticed her before. On Bet's lap sits my mom, her anger management prop still intact.

"Tabitha Mascaros," Bet says. "Size five shoe."

"Yes," Tabitha says. "You remember me?"

"Of course I do," Bet says. "You changed your name?"

"Just for the job," Tabitha says. "Everyone would have known it was me with a name like Mascaros."

(This is so not how I thought this scene would play out.)

"Did you do a show here, Tabitha?" Stella asks.

"I . . ." Tabitha looks around the room.

"Take your time," I say.

"You're being far too kind to me," Tabitha says. "I don't deserve it."

"My mom raised me to be kind," I say, pointing toward Mom on Bet's lap. "No matter what."

Tabitha looks over and acknowledges my mother with another elegant nod. My mother manages a smile—her frustration cooled by this puzzling person who clearly has good in her.

Tabitha looks at Bet with full, pleading eyes. And Bet—dear, wise Bet—begins the story for her.

"The title of the show is irrelevant; so is the year," Bet says. "All you need to know is that during technical rehearsal, Tabitha was let go."

The words *let go* cause Tabitha to flinch, ever so slightly.

"What happened?" I ask.

"Once they got the show up on the stage, the choreographer decided that Tabitha didn't blend in with the other dancers. Said she was distracting."

Distracting.

"I'm so very sorry," Stella says. "How terrible."

Tabitha looks at Stella, then at me. She smiles a bit—the first hint of a smile I've seen so far. Then she returns her gaze to Bet, as if she's waiting for her to keep telling the story.

"I knew the real reason, though," Bet says. "And I told Tabitha, because I didn't want her to think that something about her—something she couldn't change—was the reason she lost her Broadway debut."

"What was the real reason?" I ask.

"The lead actress wanted her gone," Bet says. "Tabitha was one of her understudies. The actress was a bit under the weather, so they decided to rehearse Tabitha, just to be safe. Talk spread through the theatre of how wonderful she was in the role. And that was that."

"I remember hearing this story," Stella says. "The actress was married to the director, if memory serves?"

Tabitha nods and removes her delicate glasses to wipe away a tear.

This poor woman. A jealous star threw her dream in the *spazzatura* and all these years later, she hasn't recovered.

"Can we . . . ," Tabitha begins. "Can we go out onto the stage? Just for a moment?"

"Of course," Stella says. "Let's all go."

Stella leads the way into the wings, with Tabitha following closely and quietly behind. Bet carries me and my mom in her housecoat pockets. Stella walks from the stage left wings onto the stage; the curtain is up, so we're looking out into the empty house.

There's something about being onstage between shows. The house is all clean—our hardworking staff has picked up after the audience members who don't understand that the floor of the house isn't a garbage can, and my brothers have collected their evening snacks. The house lights are on, so the lighting is really cozy and warm. Most of our company either naps in their dressing rooms or goes out to eat between shows, so the theatre, overall, is very quiet. It's as if the theatre is taking a nap, too. There's a peace to the whole thing. A sense of serenity. Like a snowstorm or a summer rain. A time to recharge and start anew.

"I . . . I haven't seen things from this perspective in a very long time," Tabitha says. "But I've never forgotten the first time I walked out on this stage."

"How old were you when you made your—" I stop myself. "When you were cast in the show?"

"Twenty-five," Tabitha says. "But when I first walked out on this stage I was twelve. A friend of my mother's was in *A Little Night Music,* and she brought us backstage. The moment I stepped out of the wings . . . I was in love. To make my Broadway debut here, half a lifetime later . . . it all felt so perfect. I should have known."

"Known what?" I ask.

"That nothing in life is perfect. And when you feel like it is, you should be prepared for something to go wrong. Nothing works out the way we hope it will."

A bit of quick math, and I've determined that this woman is in her late fifties. The heartbreak she experienced in this theatre happened thirty-ish years ago. For longer than a lot of my castmates have been alive, Tabitha Mascaros (aka T. Mason) has been broken. And broken people? They're often cruel. This all makes so much sense.

"Tabitha, if you don't mind my asking, why didn't you try again?"

I know what the answer is going to be. But I need to hear her say it. She needs to say it. Out loud. In this space. For us to hear, for the ghosts to hear, for her to hear.

"I did try, at first," Tabitha says. "I went to auditions. But it was as if I had lost the thing that made me special.

I didn't dance like I had before. . . . And hearing people whisper about me . . . well, there's only so much a young woman can take. I very quickly realized that it was just easier to give up."

I hop out of Bet's hands and scurry down her dress, across my beloved stage, and to the tiny feet of a tiny, broken human. She sits down next to me with such ease I suspect she still secretly takes dance classes. Faster than you can say "And the Tony goes to *Hadestown,*" I'm on the knee of the human who has, for the last two months, made it her mission to destroy my dream. The woman who called me names and spun lies about the goings-on in this building is stroking my head gently and kindly. This is who she is. The rest is just her armor. The armor she wears to keep from getting hurt again.

"If we give up," I say, "we'll never know what could have been."

I look upstage. Bet is cradling my mom, and they're

both crying. Even Stella is a bit teary—it's just a polished, composed cry, the kind we'd expect from Mary Poppins or royalty.

Movement from Tabitha turns me back to her. She's weeping. Heaving sobs. Jayne was telling me the other day that her acting teacher says we all carry around pockets of pain. That, onstage, through our characters, we're able to use that pain and then let it go. Tabitha Mascaros has been carrying around this pocket of pain for more than half of her life. And here, right here at the site of her heartache, she is finally letting it go.

"I'm so sorry," she says. "I'm so sorry for all the things I wrote."

"It's okay," I say.

"I took a job at the paper as a proofreader, just to make ends meet. When the man who ran the paper found out I had been fired from a Broadway show, he decided I was the perfect person to write a gossip column about the theatre."

"He took advantage of your misfortune," Mom says.

"It was his idea to make me anonymous," Tabitha says. "He thought it would sell more papers."

"He was right about that," Bet says.

"At first, I was playing a part. I put all my frustration and anger and jealousy into the role. But over the years, it became who I was. I became mean. And every time I tried to quit, every time I tried to write something kind or complimentary, I remembered the moment, right over there." She points offstage right, to the base of the stairs that lead to the ensemble female dressing room. "That's where they told me I was fired. Every time I would try to start fresh, I would think of that, and I'd become T. Mason again. The idea of a mouse achieving what I had worked so hard for, on the stage where it was supposed to happen to me, it was just . . . it was just too much for my heart to handle. You making history here, Lulu . . . it made me even more cruel than I usually am."

"Not you," I say. "T. Mason."

"Sometimes our characters bleed a bit too far into our real life," Stella says. "It's happened to me, too."

Tabitha smiles in a subtle, almost embarrassed way. Then her attention is pulled once again to the base of the stairs offstage right. The place where Tabitha Mascaros lost the piece of herself that made her shine.

"It's never too late to start over," I say.

"We'll see," Tabitha says.

She pulls a very familiar-looking handkerchief out of her coat pocket and blows her nose. "All these years and I still have this," Tabitha says to Bet, holding up the handkerchief. "You gave it to me and said, 'Don't waste your tears on jealousy—'"

"'—tomorrow will be brighter,'" Bet finishes, repeating what she said all those years ago.

"But it wasn't," Tabitha says. "I let them take my dream. And from then on, everything was dark."

It's at this moment that the crew decides to start

testing the lights. Pink and blue and warm yellow shine down onto Tabitha. A spotlight clicks into place.

Tabitha stands and closes her eyes. She tilts her head back, absorbing the warmth.

I know it sounds a little "woo-woo," as Jodie Howard would say, but I swear to you, it's as if Tabitha is healing right before our eyes.

And then, she takes a bow.

"That felt good," she says.

"It's the best feeling in the whole wide world," I say.

"I understand why you're fighting so hard to save it," she says. "And I'm going to help you do it."

THEATRE THOUGHTS with T. Mason

I have been lying to you for years, New York. But no more. From here on out, it's truth time. Yesterday, after the curtain came down on the matinee, I paid a visit to the Shubert Theatre. There, I was greeted by costars Stella James and Lulu the Mouse—performers I have repeatedly wronged with my words. And yet, they welcomed me with open arms. They didn't yell. Didn't call me names. Didn't attack. They listened. They cared. They asked: Why? New York, I will never reveal to you all the details of my past, nor will I reveal my identity. These truths are mine to keep. But I will admit that experiences of mine—theatrical experiences—broke me in such a way that I turned into the columnist you know today as T. Mason. I have spent the last three decades gossiping and telling tall tales, and it has been exhausting. So I am done. This is my last column. My new friends at the Shubert showed me the light, and I have decided to start anew. I leave you with this: A mouse is currently performing nightly at the Shubert, alongside one of the most talented companies I've ever seen. If you do not see this show, New York, you will regret it for the rest of your life. Do yourself a favor and buy a ticket. Buy two, buy three. Bring your spouse, your child, your friend—or your enemy. And escape into the world that Lulu and company have created. It is a world I would live in forever if I could.

CHAPTER
TWENTY-TWO

SIX DAYS LATER, JODIE APPEARS IN THE DOORWAY of her and H.H.'s dressing room, clad neck to ankle in jean. She shakes her head slowly from side to side and says, "Well, I have news, but it's not good."

"What's wrong?" I ask. Because things have been going well, Team. Really well. *We were sold out on Sunday* well. My castmates still frequent the TKTS booth before each show, *On Broadway with Bernard Bradshaw* has been re-airing constantly, and T. Mason's apology column seems to have given many of her loyal readers permission to like me. Who knows which factor is making the most difference—it's really not important. What's important is, audiences are showing up.

So in this moment, I really hope Jodie isn't here to tell us—

"*Apartment* isn't getting picked up to series," Jodie says.

Whew. What a relief. (I mean that in the least selfish way possible.)

"Oh, I'm so sorry, Jodie," H.H. says. She gives her face a spritz with some schmancy rose water she bought at a spa in Tribeca. "Did they give a reason?"

"Other shows tested more positively." Jodie collapses onto their *chaise longue*. "Remind me never to do network television again."

H.H. rolls her eyes and says, "I'll remind you."

"Company, this is your Half-Hour call," Pete's voice pipes over the monitor. "And after the show tonight, please remain onstage after the curtain comes down for a meeting with the producers and a special guest. Half Hour, please. Half Hour."

My stomach just flipped. If it competed in the Olympics, it would be sporting a gold medal right now.

"Well, when one door closes, another opens," Jodie says. She pops up out of the chaise longue, throws her arms in the air, gazes up at the heavens (well, the ceiling, actually), and proclaims, "Thank you, theatre gods!"

Does Jodie's pivot turn from sad to happy mean what I think it means? I won't dare say it out loud, but you know what I'm thinking, Team. You know what I'm thinking!

"Let's not count our chickens, my dear," H.H. says. "For all we know, Oprah's in the audience and marketing wants a group picture with her."

And . . . deflate. Balloon pop. Knocked off a high shelf. *Plop.*

"Well, I suppose it could be anything," Jodie says, "but I'm hoping it's—"

"Don't say it!" I basically scream. "Don't jinx it, Jodie. For the love of *My Fair Lady,* please don't jinx it!"

I've never known Jodie Howard to take as long of a pause as she does. She's used to delivering the anxiety, not receiving it.

"Mouse got your tongue, Ms. Howard?" H.H. says. "It's all right, Tiny. No one is jinxing anything."

"Come here to me, young lady," Jodie says. "Let's take a breath. You're supposed to be the calm one around here, doll."

I scurry over to Jodie and she puts her hands down to the floor so I can step into them like they're an elevator. Then, she lifts her hands, and up I go, until we're face-to-face. "It will all work out," she says. "Do you hear me? Oprah, or the thing we're all hoping it is. It will all work out."

———◇———

THE CURTAIN COMES DOWN ON TUESDAY NIGHT'S BLUR of a show, and here we all are. Full makeup, full costumes, slightly droopy wigs—and we're just sort of standing here.

Waiting. The anticipation is possibly killing me; I've had a pain in my stomach since Half Hour that's probably an ulcer.

Jayne and I are huddled together with everyone else who just performed; H.H. handed me over to Jayne, post-bow, like she knew it was what Jayne and I needed in this very moment. Milly and Olivia are over onstage right. My parents and brothers are huddled over onstage left atop Pete's call desk, and Bet, Jeremiah, Chris, and the rest of the crew are dispersed throughout the crowd. We're all here for each other. No matter what. No matter what the news. (We know it's not Oprah because audience members would definitely have tried to take pictures of her and we would have seen their camera flashes. A friendly reminder: no photos in the theatre, even if Oprah's there.)

I really do think it's what I want it to be, Team. But as we've learned, anything's possible. Good or bad or in between.

Producer with Bangs arrives onstage first, followed by Male Producer, then Producer with Glasses. I see Male Producer signal to my brother—a tip-of-the-hat kind of move, which I can only interpret as a positive thing.

Behind the producers is a familiar face we haven't seen in a very long time. It's Samantha, our director. A wave of energy moves through the company as we all clock Samantha's presence and conjecture as to its meaning.

The seas part to make room for our four bosses, who circle up center stage around Stella. Stella, whose poker face is still on point; I have absolutely no idea what she's thinking.

I can't look out into the house to wish on a ceiling star, because the curtain is down. So I do the next best thing and look up to the stage's ceiling, which is dotted with lights. I make a silent wish.

Please let us stay open.

Please let us be the first—

—the first Broadway company to save our show.

When I open my eyes, I spot Dan and Artie up on the fly floor; Dan nods and Artie shoots me a thumbs-up.

"It's lovely to see you all again," Producer with Glasses says.

"As you can see, we've brought a special guest with us today," Male Producer says. "Samantha, the floor is yours."

"The *stage*, you mean," Producer with Bangs says. We all laugh, though this quip really isn't witty or funny. But it's important to laugh when your boss expects you to laugh.

"Hello, everyone!" Samantha says. "How I have missed you."

We collectively throw back a few configurations of "We've missed you, too," and then promptly silence ourselves, lest we miss what Samantha is about to say.

"I am so proud of this show, and what it has become." She looks at me when she says this, which is . . . wonderful.

"And to see you putting so much effort into trying to save it? Hours and hours at the TKTS booths, in the alley, and on social media? I am so proud and so inspired."

The producers are standing behind Samantha, nodding along in unison, like they're her backup singers. This is all feeling super positive, but, really, who knows? Show biz is a game that changes its rules each time you finally learn how to play.

"Unfortunately, just because we put a lot of effort into something doesn't mean it will pay off," Samantha says.

Half of this company just sprouted a stress pimple; I'm sure of it. A wave of disappointment passes over us like a Harry Potter Death Eater. Why would they gather us all here if the news wasn't good? Could they possibly think that we just want to hear they're proud of us for trying?

Samantha links arms with Stella, who says, "But sometimes, it does."

Wait, what?

"If T. Mason can admit to being wrong, then so can we," Producer with Glasses says.

Is this happening?

Producer with Bangs hands Stella a piece of paper that says CLOSING NOTICE on it.

It's happening.

"Stella, if you'll please do the honors?"

Stella isn't one for a gimmick, but she plays along this time and rips the paper in half. "We're staying open, everyone."

Cheers. Applause. Tears. Because . . . we did it.

We did it.

Everyone's hugging. H.H. hugs Jodie and Jodie screams, "It's a miracle!" Then H.H. turns and hugs Lisa Logan, who looks shocked but thrilled. Dancers are skillfully jumping up and down practically in unison, and Dan and Artie are up on the fly floor hooting and hollering like the Mets just won the World Series.

"We owe a special thanks to our Benji," Stella says. She waves Benji over. He scurries down the edge of Pete's stage left post and makes his way to center stage, the company applauding him the whole way. "A brilliant idea," Stella says. "We couldn't have done it without you."

"It was so crazy it just . . . worked!" Benji says. He's not a British butler, he's not Max Bialystock, he's not a cowboy. He's Benji, my brother and my friend and a guy who cares just as much about the theatre as I do, just in a very different way.

Everyone laughs, and our oldest castmate, Joe, starts singing "For He's a Jolly Good Fellow." The rest of us join in. We sing it beautifully—in harmony, of course—and it's a moment I'll never forget. It's amazing what can happen when people (and mice) work together toward a common goal. Even if we hadn't saved the show, I'm sure glad we tried.

But we did save the show! Wheeeeeee!!!!!

"Champagne and sparkling apple cider in the basement once everyone gets out of costume," Pete hollers. I'm not kidding you when I say Susie does a high kick up to her ear, which might as well be the GIF for how we're all feeling.

Milly and Olivia make their way over to me and Jayne and we hug it out.

"Now I'll get to go on again!" Olivia says.

"Olivia," Milly says.

"What?" Olivia says. "It would be surprising if Jayne didn't miss another show."

"You know what, Olivia?" Jayne says. "You're right. In fact, now that we're staying open, I'll have to miss a show in May, to film another scene with Meryl."

"I'll go tell Pete!" Olivia says. She runs off toward Pete with Milly following behind her, because an understudy telling a stage manager that she'll be going on is the opposite of how things work.

"She's excited," Jayne says. "I can't really blame her."

"I can't either," I say. "I'm so excited I could burst."

"Please don't," Jayne says. "Audiences want to see Lulu the Mouse. And I need my costar/best friend combo."

"I promise not to burst," I say. "But I can't promise not to sing extra full-out during the matinee tomorrow."

"Do it," Jayne says. "The people want to hear you sing!"

"They do," I say. "It's really something, isn't it?"

"Nothing's impossible now," Jayne says. "You taught me that. You and Benji and Stella. Everyone. When the show finally does close, or I get too tall for the part or whatever, I'll leave here knowing anything is possible."

Do you hear Jayne, dear reader? Hear her, here and now. Anything is possible. *Anything.*

"Thanks," I say. "Just . . . thanks."

"You're welcome," Jayne says. "Now. Let's go get some of that sparkling cider! I bet there's some sort of dessert, too. I heard Rosa say a delivery had arrived."

CHAPTER
TWENTY-THREE

HERE WAS RED VELVET CAKE FROM AMY'S
Bread and a chocolate chip pie from Little Pie
Company. Cookies from Schmackary's. A mystery buyer (whose last name is probably James) ordered pizza from Joe's Pizza over on Broadway. My brothers were in heaven. And so was I—and not just because of the perfect combination that is cheese and chocolate—but because I was with my favorite people, celebrating the fact that we're not going anywhere.

For now, at least.

But for now is all we have, I suppose. And this brush with closing made us all more thankful for it. For each high note, each pin curl, each *shuffle ball change,* each Places call. We can't take anything for granted, dear reader. Dear Team.

And right now? I'm up onstage. Just me and the ghost light. Just like I was the evening of my Broadway debut and post-debut party. I love my theatre family and my mouse family, but sometimes a gal needs a moment by herself to process things and recharge.

I lay down on the base of the ghost light, curling my tail around its stand so I'm tucked in and cozy.

"Come out, ghosts," I say. "Please come out." I make this request, from time to time, because as we've learned, anything is possible. A mouse summoning a theatre ghost doesn't seem like too far of a reach.

"I'm not a ghost," H.H. says. "Yet." She struts across the stage with her legs for days and sits down next to me. "When I shed my human form, I can't decide if I'll haunt this theatre or the Belasco."

"Umm . . . how is that even a question?" I ask.

"The Belasco is exquisite," H.H. says. "Tiffany lamps all over the place. Very forgiving lighting."

"You won't need forgiving lighting when you're a ghost," I say.

"We don't know anything for certain until it happens," H.H. says. "Now that you've been all the way to Times Square, perhaps your parents will let me sneak you over to the Belasco. It's something you need to see for yourself."

"I'd love that," I say. "But the Shubert will always be my home."

"I know, Tiny," H.H. says. "Home is where the heart is, hmm?" She giggles a bit. "My sister gave me an absolutely hideous pillow with that saying embroidered on it. Spot-on sentiment, but *hideous*."

"Bring it to the basement," I say. "My brothers are always looking for a place to relax post-snack."

"Tomorrow," H.H. says. "Then I'll bring you upstairs with me for our preshow."

"Perfect," I say.

"I'm glad it's not over yet," she says.

"Me too," I say.

H.H. pats me on the head and heads to the stage left wings, bound for the dressing room and then her home on the Upper West Side.

I'm so lucky to have such a short commute. Under two minutes from center stage to my cozy basement nest.

I'll head downstairs in a few, but for now I'm more than content curled up on the base of the ghost light. All alone. Just me and the ghosts.

———————◇———————

I WAKE UP TO THE SOUND OF HIGH-HEELED FOOTSTEPS. I must have only dozed off for a few minutes; there's no way my mom would let me stay up here all night.

The footsteps get closer and closer. A familiar rhythm. Calm, measured, confident.

It's Stella.

She makes her way to center stage, and while I would love nothing more than one-on-one time with Tony winner Stella James, I'm very aware that she's probably looking for a little alone time as well, so until she sees me, I won't say a word. I'll be . . . as quiet as a mouse.

Stella looks out into the empty house for a few counts of eight. And then she says, "Thank you."

I don't think she's talking to me. I'm fairly certain she's talking to the theatre itself. This magical building that for over one hundred years has been so full of love and energy and blood, sweat, and tears, that it's practically a living, breathing organism at this point. She's thanking it for helping us. For being a place where dreams can come true and stay true.

She puts her hand to her heart, closes her eyes, and says, "Thank you," again. Then she slowly exits offstage left to her dressing room.

Everything comes in threes, dear reader. You know I believe this.

So I stand up, make my way to center stage, and say, "Thank you."

I know you're going to think I'm nuts, but I swear to you, I hear the Shubert say, "You're welcome, Lulu."

I'm welcome. Here. Onstage at the Shubert Theatre. On Broadway.

Me.

Lulu the Broadway Mouse.

I take in the empty house for one more glorious moment, then head down to my nest and a good night's sleep.

We have two shows tomorrow, after all.

And I wouldn't trade that fact for anything in the world.

The End

A Glossary of (Mostly) Theatre Terms
by Lulu the Broadway Mouse

Actors' Equity Association: The union that represents stage actors and stage managers. Members pay dues, and those dues mean the union representatives will negotiate contracts that keep members safe, well-paid, and in possession of important benefits like health insurance and a retirement fund. You might see AEA mentioned in an actor's Playbill biography. AEA = Actors' Equity Association.

Bell kick: A type of dance move/jump where a dancer's two heels come together to the right or left of the dancer's body to create the shape of a bell.

Booking: When you get the job you auditioned for—you booked it! It applies to television and film as well as the theatre. It's just a universal show biz term for getting the gig.

Broadway Dance Center: A dance school on West Forty-Fifth Street between Eighth and Ninth Avenues (a few doors down from the Al Hirschfeld Theatre). They also have a location uptown on West Sixty-Fifth Street that's just for children and teenagers.

Button: The clear, intentional end to a scene or musical number. You can hear a button (if you're listening to a cast recording!) and you can also see it in action, as a physical movement. (YouTube "All That Jazz," the opening number of *Chicago*. The end of the number is an excellent example of movement and music coming together to form a perfect button.)

Call board: This usually hangs not far from the stage door entrance. At the Shubert, ours is at the foot of the staircase that leads up to the dressing rooms, right around the corner from where Rosa sits. On the call board hangs the ever-important sign-in sheet and any notes or notices that stage management or the producers post. For example: when an understudy is on, there'll be a notice about it on the call board.

Calling out: Saying you're going to be absent for a performance (or a few performances). "I have a splitting headache, so I'm calling out for tonight's show."

Casting director: A human whose job it is to find performers who are right for roles and to present them to the creative team, aka the director, choreographer, producers, composers . . . you get it. Step one of an audition process is often an audition in front of just the casting director, though once a performer has a reputation for strong work, they'll often be brought straight to the creative team.

Character shoes: A high-heeled (but not too high-heeled), sturdy shoe worn for rehearsals and onstage. The shoe usually has a bit of a bend in its arch so a performer can point his or her toe.

Cuts: In the theatre, when something is there but it needs to go, it is cut. When a dancer is cut from an audition, that means they're not asked to stay and dance again or to sing—and they will most likely not get the part. A song or a scene is cut from a show when it no longer serves the plot. You'll hear movie directors yell, "Cut!" when they want to stop filming, but you'll hear theatre directors say, "We need to cut ten minutes off of this show because it is too darn long."

Ditty bag: A mesh bag that belongs to each performer and that at the beginning of a performance holds the performer's clean laundry—underwear, socks, bras, and such—and then holds that same laundry, but dirty, postshow. It's a way for my mom and Bet (and other wardrobe employees) to wash this type of laundry without having to actually touch it. Plus, it keeps everything organized.

Giving notice: Letting the powers that be (like the producers and stage management) know that you're going to be leaving the show permanently. You usually give notice a few weeks before you want to leave to give the production time to find a replacement.

Grosses: The amount of money a show makes in ticket sales. The **NUT** is removed from this amount, resulting in the show's **PROFIT** or **NET**. Fun fact: Playbill.com posts all the Broadway grosses each Monday afternoon!

Guest star: A character on an episode of a television show that plays a big part in a particular episode but may or may not come back for future episodes. An example of a guest star is the person who committed the crime on an episode of *Law & Order*.

Hand-tied wig: A hair artist uses teeny, tiny hooks (kind of like a crochet needle's) to delicately attach real human hair to a mesh cap of sorts—a mesh cap that has been measured to fit a specific performer's head—eventually creating the beautiful wigs you see up onstage. Probably close to forty to fifty hours of work go into each wig, which is why they're very expensive. The even more technical term is **VENTILATED**. "A hair artist ventilates a wig."

Mark Fisher Fitness: A really fun gym frequented by members of the theatre community. (I've never been, of course, but H.H. loves it there, so I've heard all about it.)

Marquee: The big sign (usually made up of sparkling lights!) that displays the name of a theatre, the show that's currently playing, and sometimes the name of the show's star.

Midtown turnaround: I'm not sure who first introduced me to this term, but I'd venture to guess it was Jodie Howard because, bless her, she loves to gossip. It means that you'd better look around while in the theatre district (aka Midtown Manhattan) before you tell a story or gossip or complain or whatever. Because the odds of someone who shouldn't hear what you're saying being around to hear it are pretty high in this tiny neighborhood on our dear tiny island of Manhattan.

Name plaque/name placard: A sturdy rectangle that hangs along with other sturdy rectangles in the box office of a theatre and sports the name of a member of the company. Basically, all of the rectangles together form a cast list, but what makes these placards extra special is that they can move, so they can be used on a secondary board—the **AT THIS PERFORMANCE** board—that lets an audience know if an understudy is on for the performance. Name plaques/placards also often hang on dressing room doors to clearly show who's inside!

Nut: Also known as the **WEEKLY OPERATING COSTS**, a show's nut is how much money it costs to run. (Running costs include but are most certainly not limited to salaries, advertising, insurance. . . .)

Open call: A type of audition that was not arranged by an agent, where a performer shows up, sometimes waits for a long time, and then auditions. (Hopefully. There are only so many hours in a day and, needless to say, there are a lot of people who want to audition for the theatre!)

Personal day: On Broadway, all actors are allotted a few of these a year. An actor asks to use up one of their personal days if they need to miss a show for a friend's wedding or a day working on a commercial or something like that. Or if they just need a mental health day, which is totally allowed!

Possible recurring: When a guest star will maybe return. Apparently, hearing "possible recurring" is a really big deal to an actor. (As evidenced by Jodie Howard's elation upon booking her role on *Apartment*.)

Premium ticket pricing: A show's most expensive tickets because they're in a theatre's best seats.

Put-in: A rehearsal for an understudy or someone new to a role. It's a rehearsal that happens during the day, in front of an empty house, and the show is run all the way through with most sets, costumes, and cast members present. It's a way for a performer to have as close to a real experience in a role and a show as possible, without the stress of performing in front of a live, paying audience.

Recurring role: When a guest star comes back in future episodes. An example of a recurring role is a judge on *Law & Order*.

Show report: Written up by stage management after each show, this document contains details such as whether an understudy performed, anyone was injured, someone forgot a line, a cell phone went off in the audience, what time the show started and ended . . . that sort of thing. The show report is sent to important people who aren't in the building every day, like a show's producers.

Swing: A cast member who is an understudy for many other performers. (Sometimes one swing will "cover" an entire ensemble. That could be a dozen people!) A swing doesn't have his or her own track, so they only perform when an actor is absent—or on for another role, if that actor is an understudy. When a swing is not performing, they're usually watching the show or "trailing" one of the actors they cover, to make sure they stay sharp on the details of each track. Being a swing requires a lot of memorization and precision.

Television pilot: This is like a television show's audition to be a full-fledged series! Traditionally, television pilots are filmed in the winter and it's decided in the late spring whether the pilot will become a television show with lots of episodes that audiences will actually see. (Pilots are only aired if the full show gets **PICKED UP TO SERIES**.) I say "traditionally" because, according to Jodie Howard, "Things are changing in television faster than my hair color in the eighties!"

Throat Coat tea: The tea of choice for many singers. It's an excellent addition to a preshow routine.

TKTS *booth*: A booth in Times Square run by TDF (aka the Theatre Development Fund) that sells discounted tickets* to Broadway and off-Broadway shows. Tickets are only available for that day's performance. So, if you're seeing a Tuesday night show, go to the booth sometime on Tuesday, and you're good. If you're seeing a show on a two-show day, go to the TKTS booth prior to the performance you wish to see. (You can't get tickets to a Saturday night show at noon because Saturday's two o'clock tickets will be sold first, is what I'm saying. Traditionally, shows do two shows on Wednesdays and Saturdays, though every show's schedule is different, so make sure to check a show's schedule before you buy tickets. *Phantom of the Opera,* for example, has two shows on Thursday.) There are also TKTS booths up by Lincoln Center and down at the South Street Seaport.

Also look for discounted tickets on apps called TodayTix and BroadwayBox. And make sure to check out a show's website for information on its specific discount options, like student discounts and digital lotteries.

Track: All those names on the sign-in sheet or the board in the lobby have a track. Stella's track consists of just one role, while many ensemble tracks consist of a half dozen roles all played by one human. (I used Harper as an example earlier. Harper plays a maid, a dinner guest, and a passerby. Those three roles put together = Harper's track.) When an understudy or swing goes on for someone's track, that basically means they're doing exactly what the missing performer normally does each night—like they're walking in their footsteps. A **SPLIT TRACK** means one performer is going on for two tracks! Split tracks will happen when there are too many people out and not enough people to fill the tracks. It doesn't happen often, but when it does, it's thrilling and super impressive.

Hungry? Here Are Some Eateries Mentioned in This Book

5 NAPKIN BURGER: located on Ninth Avenue between Forty-Fourth and Forty-Fifth Streets, their menu consists of . . . wait for it . . . burgers! And salads and appetizers and onion rings so crunchy just the idea of them makes my mouth water. Oh, and milk-shakes. (I should know better than to write about food whilst hungry.)

JOE'S PIZZA: the original one is down on Carmine Street in the West Village but they just opened one on Broadway between Fortieth and Forty-First Streets. Seeing an 8:00 pm show and it's currently 7:30 and you still need to eat? Grab a slice and get thee to the theatre with more than enough time to spare! (But for the love of mozzarella cheese, please do not eat your pizza while inside the theatre.)

KODAMA SUSHI: located directly across from the Al Hirschfeld Theatre on Forty-Fifth Street just west of Eighth Avenue, this restaurant is a great place to catch a bite before a show if you're in the mood for Japanese food! (I've sampled many of their menu items, as it's also a popular takeout destination for many of my castmates.)

LITTLE PIE COMPANY: a bakery on Forty-Third Street between Ninth and Tenth Avenues. We often order their pies and cakes for company members' birthdays. Just go and thank me later.

SCHMACKARY'S: you heard all about it in Chapter Twelve so you know Schmackary's = a cookie shop on Forty-Fifth Street just east of Ninth Avenue, and you also know that you must, must, must visit it when you're in town.

THAT'S ALL SHE WROTE FOR NOW, TEAM! (MORE SOON, I hope.)

With endless applause,

Lucy Louise

aka Lulu the Broadway Mouse

Acknowledgments

IT FEELS AS THOUGH I WAS JUST WRITING THE ACKNOWL-edgments for *Lulu the Broadway Mouse*, but that was almost two years ago?! Time flies when you're playing make-believe for a living, and when your work life and *life* life are graced by the greatest group of humans a gal could ask for. The following is a sampling of those who help me when it comes to life and Lulu. (If I thanked you in the acknowledgments of *Lulu the Broadway Mouse*, consider yourself thanked again.)

Entrance and exit applause for "Team Lulu" at Running Press Kids and Hachette Book Group who made Lulu's debut a success and made her sequel a reality. Julie Matysik, Adrienne Szpyrka, Valerie Howlett, Allison Cohen, Frances J. Soo Ping Chow, Michael Clark, Cassie Drumm, Tracy Daniels, Casey Blackwell, Christina Palaia, Christine Farrell, Charles McCrorey: thank you for making this process so seamless and dreamy. Working with you all is like working with a grammatically correct, cozy hug. Truly, what could be better?

A mid-show standing ovation for the booksellers, educators, and Kid Lit world rock stars who championed Lulu's debut and encouraged an encore.

A spotlight on Bridget, Greg, and Connor Mills, to whom I often turned when I needed to be reminded of how things work backstage (because they were all employed on Broadway while I was writing this book!), and who were especially helpful in spreading the word of the first book's debut.

Bravo, Erwin Madrid! Thank you for your illustrations and cover art, which so beautifully and accurately capture the magic of the theatre and Lulu's world.

Endless applause for Linda Epstein—my agent, my friend, my Fairy God-Yente. Thank you for believing in me and Lulu, and for your years of hard work and support.

Thank you to my theatre family, for the inspiration.

Thank you to my parents and my family and friends, for your support and love, and for organizing and attending a book party that was basically a small wedding (one year after a real wedding). Speaking of weddings . . . thanks, Husband. You're wonderful.

Lulu and I do love to quote musicals, so here's something from *The King and I*. "The children, the children, I'll not forget the children . . ." Thank you, dear readers, for choosing to spend your time with Lulu & Company. And for spending time with me; visiting you in school is one of the great privileges of my life. (And lately I've been lucky enough to perform with a handful of Broadway's current kids, which is such a joy!) A question many of you ask is why I decided to write about Lulu. There are many reasons, but the short answer is: I grew up, life got in the way, and I forgot why I wanted to be in show business in the first place. Writing about Lulu and her world helps me to remember.

(The reason why is love.)

The Show Must Go On and *Lulu the Broadway Mouse* are brought to you straight from my heart. It's a heart that has belonged to the theatre since before I could spell the word, and I'm happy to report that it has expanded in size to make room for writing books. Thank you to everyone who makes my playing make-believe a real thing. It's a wonderful way to live a life.

About the Author

JENNA GAVIGAN IS THE AUTHOR OF THE MIDDLE-grade novel *Lulu the Broadway Mouse*. A professional actress for more than half her life, she's appeared on Broadway, on a gaggle of television shows, in a handful of movies, and on stages east and west. A fourth-generation New Yorker, Jenna graduated with a BA in creative writing from Columbia University, where she focused on fiction, television, and screenwriting. Like Lulu, Jenna made her Broadway debut at the Shubert Theatre. (Though, sadly, she doesn't live there.) Visit her at iamjennagavigan.com and on Twitter and Instagram @Jenna_Gavigan.